STRIPES
PUBLISHING
An imprint of
Magi Publications
1 The Coda Centre,
189 Munster Road,
London SW6 6AW

A paperback original
First published in Great Britain in 2008
Text copyright © Liz Elwes, 2008
ISBN: 978-1-84715-054-7

The right of Liz Elwes
to be identified as
the author of this
work has been
asserted by her in
accordance with the
Copyright, Designs
and Patents
Act, 1988.

A CIP catalogue
record for this book
is available from
the British Library.

Printed and bound
in Belgium.

To Giles, William, Alice, Thomas and Jamie.
All my family and friends and Frank Read for their inspiration.
To Jane Harris and everyone at Stripes for all their hard work.

Amy

Liz Elwes

Stripes

"A pony?"

"Yes."

"A *pony*?!"

"Yes."

"A po—"

"Oh for goodness' sake, Amy! I wish I'd never told you."

"*I* wish you'd never told me!"

"You *did ask*."

"Yes, Mum, I *did* ask. But that was because I thought you were going to say that you had

named me after one of your best friends at school, or the heroine of your favourite book or something *normal* like that…"

"Amy is a *very* pretty name."

"That's not the point, Mum! The fact is that the Amy I was named after was a bit on the shaggy side and liked munching hay. Was Dad in on this brilliant idea, too?"

"He thought Amy was a great name, and she *was* a very sweet…"

I put my hands over my ears. "Mum, you're making it *worse*."

"I'm joking! It wasn't just the pony thing," Mum continued, exasperated. "Amy is originally a French name and it means—"

"I don't want to hear it. Knowing my luck it probably means 'big teeth and likes eating grass'."

Mum put up her hands in surrender. "OK, I won't say another word. But why don't you ask someone when we're on holiday in France?" She glanced at her watch. "Oh no! Look at the time; I've got to catch the post office before it closes." She dashed down to the kitchen and reappeared two minutes

later clutching her keys and handbag. "Please could you keep an eye on Jack for me? I won't be long."

"Mu-um! Can't you see I'm in the middle of packing?"

"Surely you can't be thinking of taking any more than that!" she gasped, eyeing my overflowing suitcase. "We'll need a trailer."

"Oh too hilarious, Mum."

We were all going to France for our summer holiday. Which didn't sound that bad. But we weren't going to be staying in some glamorous villa, with a pool and stony steps leading down to a sandy beach. Oh no. We were staying on a campsite, in the middle of *nowhere*. For two whole weeks. But I still wanted to look my best. Sasha says a girl should always make an effort with her appearance as you never know who you might meet. I didn't feel there would be much chance of meeting anyone where we were going, though.

We were leaving at the crack of dawn the next day, and I wanted time to myself to phone Sasha for one last gossip, and then get on with getting ready.

Sweet Dreams

Looking after my younger brother was going to seriously cut into my schedule. I checked the pink Post-it note on my mirror.

Things to do before holiday:

1. Exfoliate legs to silky smoothness. Use porridge-oats method as described in mag.

2. Apply fake tan for sun-kissed effect.

3. Deep condition hair in preparation for drying effects of sun. Use olive oil – mag again.

4. Apply newly-purchased and very expensive purifying face pack.

5. Put tea bags on eyes to bring out sparkly gorgeousness.

I heard the front door slam shut and sighed. I'd just have to hope Jack would carry on playing with his train set in his room. But no, three seconds after I had dialled Sasha's number, his little blond head appeared at my door.

"Go away!" I hissed. He ignored me and clambered on to my bed.

"Can you make room for Spiderman Monkey," he asked, stuffing a soft, grey bundle with a grubby, red hanky tied round its neck under

my duvet. Sasha's phone was still ringing. I hoped she was in.

"Don't do that! It's dirty!" I yelped.

"Amy? I hope that's you, otherwise someone very weird is calling me."

"Ooops! Sorry, Sasha, it's only Jack and his grubby monkey."

"Are you all set for your holiday, then?" Sasha asked excitedly. "I've been packing for days. How many pairs of shorts have you got?" She then described every item of clothing she was taking, before getting on to her favourite subject: boys. "There's a disco every night at our hotel and I can't wear the same thing twice. I bet I'm going to hit Bianca's target a thousand times over."

"Lucky you," I sighed.

"Got to go now," she cried. "Mum's yelling. Have the best time you can and don't worry about the target. You won't be the only one who doesn't make it. That girl is crazy."

Everyone knew Bianca; she was in another class in my year, but she was so loud and outrageous the whole school knew her. Last week at break

she had breathlessly skidded into our classroom, clung on to the door frame, catching her breath, and announced that we all needed to know that she had officially declared this summer the "Summer of Snog".

"It is the sacred duty of every girl in this year group to kiss at least *one boy* before they come back next term. OK?" She gave us all a stern glare. "Got that? Good." Then she beamed. "Got to go. Two more classrooms to tell." And she was off.

I've told Sasha I've kissed a boy. I told her that I kissed Dale O'Brien at the last school dance. But the truth is that when he suddenly lurched forward during the slow song, I lost my nerve and ducked, and he slurped my forehead instead. And then he was too embarrassed to try again and that was that. I was relieved more than anything else. Dale is a nice boy, but he is not THE ONE. Neither is Ralph Levinson, who lives next door and is always finding excuses to come round. But when will THE ONE appear? I was almost giving up hope.

Sasha thought I was way too romantic. Always dreaming about the perfect boy. Maybe she was

right; I know most of my teachers would agree with her on the dreamy bit. It was all very well for her; she was going to the Maldives, where boys obviously lay around all over the place in their hundreds. Not a campsite in France, where my chances of meeting great boys were practically nil. To be honest, I was not totally sure where the Maldives were, but I guessed they would be expensive and glamorous – a bit like Sasha, really.

We hadn't been friends for that long, a term and a bit. When I first started at Southwood High all my friends were my riding friends. That was in the days when I used to practically live at the stables, before the accident. I missed about a term of school afterwards, and when I returned I suppose we drifted apart from each other.

Sasha's great – really confident and funny. She's never had to pretend a slurp on the forehead was a proper kiss, and when boys are around it's impossible for anyone to get a word in edgeways. When she tosses her long, gleaming brown hair over her shoulders and fixes them with her flirty green eyes, she has them all under her spell.

Well, most of them. Baz Milton never pays her any attention. And it drives her mad.

Yesterday he was sitting on the next lunch table, ignoring her. I knew she minded about him because she always talked louder and played with her hair more when he was around, but he still never seemed to notice. We could see the back of his tall frame and blond, tousled hair. He was looking at a script.

He's going to be Romeo in our Year's production of *Romeo and Juliet* next term. Auditions were still going on, though, and I was thinking of trying for a part. Sasha had tried for Juliet, but hadn't got it, which she said just went to show what a rubbish drama teacher Miss Sands was because everyone knew she was perfect for the role. The one thing she doesn't lack is confidence; she doesn't waste her days dreaming about the one, special boy she's never even met.

Jack hopped off the bed. "I'm goin' to read now."

"Great idea! Off you go." I grabbed my magazine, thundered downstairs, raided the kitchen for olive oil and headed for the bathroom.

A few minutes later, I had rubbed the oil all over my unruly, blonde curls and wrapped a towel around my head. I put on the face pack and dashed downstairs again to get two tea bags. I held them under the tap till they were well and truly drippy and ran upstairs to my room. Then I lay on my bed, put the tea bags on my eyes and relaxed. Phew. Looking good was hard work.

I heard the padding of little feet and someone heavy breathing in my ear.

"You look funny."

"I'm making myself beautiful."

More breathing. "It's not working."

"Go away."

"I've come to read to you, Amy. You can listen while you're lying down."

I sighed. "OK then, if you must."

The bed bounced as Jack squeezed on.

"That word is 'a'." Jack had sat himself down next to me with a wriggle and jabbed firmly at the page.

I lifted a tea bag. "Yes, it is." I yawned, replacing it. "It says, 'I do not like it in *a* house...'"

I sighed. This was what it was going to be like for the next fortnight – cooped up in a tent with my five-year-old brother. With nothing to do. And only sad people, whose parents couldn't take them to the Maldives, to hang out with; certainly no one fun like Sasha…

"I can read that word, that word 'a'."

"Good for you, Jack."

Two weeks with nothing to do and surely not a hope of meeting Bianca's target … which reminded me, I must get some porridge oats to exfoliate my legs into silky smoothness.

"Everyone in the whole world can read that word. That word 'a'."

"Great, yes, they probably can, it's the easiest word there is."

I tucked an escaping tendril of hair back under the towel and prayed the oil was working its magic. I was looking forward to seeing it all shiny and glossy. My hair was important. Mum goes on about how it hides my "gorgeous blue eyes", but it covers a thin, white scar on my forehead – so it's staying. I mean it's not like boys aren't interested

in me – Sasha says it's obvious Dale still fancies me, but he's not the boy I'm waiting for in my dreams. There have to be *some* boys in France. Surely. At least one.

"Everyone in the whole world can read 'a' 'cept…"

I sighed. "Except *who*?"

"'Cept blind people."

Oh my God. Two weeks of being imprisoned with this, with no time off for good behaviour. This was surely going to be the worst summer of my life.

The worst summer of my life had already sunk lower than I could possibly have imagined. And we hadn't even arrived yet. It started with Dad getting in a huff at breakfast.

"Did you have to use the *whole* lot, Amy?" he asked, staring into the box at the few oats left at the bottom.

It was hard to know how to respond. The porridge exfoliation experiment had not been a success. The magazine had made it sound so easy: "For super-smooth skin, mix some porridge oats to a paste

with warm water and gently massage your legs." But porridge is very tricky stuff to grab hold of, and half an hour later, I was pretty unimpressed with the results, but not nearly as unimpressed as Dad, who had to spend an hour trying to unblock the plughole in the bath. Disappointed, I decided to abandon the fake tan until we got there.

Then Jack got carsick – all over me – and Dad wouldn't even stop to let me get changed. I didn't think things could get any worse. But no. Mum managed to top that lovely experience.

The midday sun had turned the temperature in the car up to "roast". We had been at a standstill on a French motorway for several hours, and the air conditioning had broken. Jack and I were lolling our tongues out of the windows like a couple of Labradors whose irresponsible owners had gone off shopping, when Mum trilled cheerily, "I've enrolled you in the campsite's Teen Club, Amy." She took a swig from her water bottle, all very casual, as if she'd said nothing special and there might actually have been some sort of discussion between us about it.

"What!" I screeched. "*Teen* Club? What Teen Club? I don't believe it, Mum! Why didn't you tell me *before*?"

"It'll be fun. You'll get to meet other kids your own age. The Levinsons sent Ralph there last year, and he loved it."

"Ralph Levinson! He gives you static-shock off his shirts. And he mouth breathes. And *he* 'loved it!'"

"Exactly!" Mum cried triumphantly. "If he can have a good time, imagine what a *brilliant* time an attractive, talented, popular girl like you will have."

"But they'll all be geeks or creeps, Mum! I'm not going!" All my worst fears about this holiday were coming true. And if the others were all going to be like Ralph, I was truly doomed.

"Rubbish. There're bound to be people you like. And the list of activities sounds fun."

"*Sounds fun!*" I snorted. When your mum says something like "sounds fun" it's time to throw yourself out of the car. Except our car wasn't moving, so the dramatic nature of the gesture would have been lost.

"What are these 'activities', then?" I asked.

"Erm… Let me see." Mum began scanning the brochure.

I craned forward. "Could *I* see, Mum? You know, *me*, the one who actually might be going to do these so-called 'activities'? The one who you didn't think to mention any of this to."

"Am I going to a club, too?" Jack piped up.

"Yes, OF COURSE you are," Mum cooed. "There's a trampoline."

"Hooray!" Jack cheered. "A tramp-amp-poline! You can be in my club, Amy. You can bounce on my tramp-amp-poline…"

I crossed my arms and stared fixedly out of the window. "I'll pass, thanks."

Mum turned and gave me one of her looks. "Amy, you know you've got to … to try things…"

I didn't reply. I knew exactly what she was getting at, and I didn't want to talk about it. But in spite of my best efforts, her words had set off a train of thought I didn't like. I wound up the window so I could put Jack's fleece against it, rested my head and pretended to go to sleep. Mum didn't mean for me to try at just anything.

She meant she wished I would try to get over what happened. But as far as I was concerned I had. I just wish she would.

She was the one who started the whole thing. She'd always wanted me to ride. She'd been a champion showjumper in her dim and distant youth and was so pleased when I fell in love with riding after my first lesson. We couldn't afford a pony of my own, but I had been entering the stable ponies in local gymkhanas and I'd been doing well.

But one misty morning last October, I was returning from a hack through the woods with Tash, the stable girl, and Polly, my best friend. Well, my best friend then. I was on Mitzi – she was the first pony I had ever ridden. She was jet black apart from a white star on her nose, and my favourite. I can remember thinking in what good spirits she was, shaking her head and breathing little, white clouds from her nostrils as we trotted back down the winding road.

We heard the cars a long time before we saw

them; the roaring engines told us that they were going fast, much too fast, but the high hedges hid them from view. Tash signalled for us to stop and pulled us back into the verge as far as we could go. Mitzi held her head up, fully alert and anxious, but stock still, as good as gold, as always.

The cars weren't slowing down; if anything they were accelerating. And then suddenly they appeared – thundering, screeching – and they weren't one behind the other, but side by side, filling the space all around us with metal and noise.

I don't remember much of what happened next, but one of the drivers lost control and swerved. Into Mitzi and me. I felt myself falling and Mitzi coming down on top of me, a sharp crack on my forehead from one of her flailing hooves as she tried to right herself, then nothing until I woke up in hospital with a broken arm and fractured skull.

They didn't tell me about Mitzi at first, but I asked and asked, and in the end they had to. She had broken both her front legs, and there was nothing anyone could do, so they had to put her down. Everyone said, "It's not your fault, it's

not your fault," but suddenly riding could never, ever be fun any more. I was scared.

Polly and my other friends, Prema and Emily, were really patient and kind; they wanted to visit, but I found seeing them too difficult. Riding was such a big part of what we used to do and talk about, and I didn't want to talk about it any more. And I didn't want to go back to the stables. Every time Mum even went near suggesting it my mouth went dry and my heart started pounding, so eventually she stopped mentioning it. Now she just makes little comments like that one. And it's so annoying because I *am* over it – I just want to be left alone to get on with my new life, that's all.

I noticed she hadn't handed me the brochure and asking for it would have involved speaking to her, so I spent the rest of the journey fuming silently and imagining the first day back at school with everyone breathlessly telling each other about how they kissed dreamy boys on moonlit beaches. Somehow, I didn't think my tales of how I'd perfected my double tuck on the trampoline would impress...

3

After approximately six hundred years, we finally arrived. We drove up a dusty road lined with slender, waving trees and stopped in front of a barrier with the name of the campsite painted on an arch above it.

"Is this to stop the inmates escaping?" I asked, as Mum and Dad clambered stiffly out of the car to check in at Reception.

"Don't be silly, it's to stop people who aren't staying at the campsite driving in and using all the wonderful facilities," Mum explained brightly.

"Yeah, that's what they tell *you*…"

"Look after Jack, we won't be long…"

"*Mum!* I'm dying here," I moaned. "I smell of sick and I think my thighs are actually welded to the seat."

"I'll get you both an ice cream while you're waiting."

"Hooray!" cheered Jack, who'd slept practically the whole way and was looking around him as if he'd just woken up in Disneyland.

I was looking around, too. To be honest, it wasn't nearly as bad as I'd expected. Instead of rows of bedraggled tents and a couple of leaning portaloos, there were shops and a bar and a little restaurant. The tents were big and in neat rows, like a little town. More interestingly, there appeared to be young people wandering about.

Out of the corner of my eye, because it's not cool to stare, I could see a group of boys messing around on bikes. They had made a ramp and were taking it in turns to do tricks. And there was no denying that one of them was completely and totally gorgeous. So gorgeous that it was very

annoying when Mum suddenly blocked my view
and thrust two vanilla cones through the window.

As soon as she'd disappeared again, I went back
to sneaking peeks at Bike Boy. He had thick, dark
hair, which kept flopping over his face, and he had
to keep taking his hand off the handlebars to push
it out of his eyes. He was wearing a battered pair
of knee-length, navy shorts and a faded red T-shirt,
which showed off his dark tan.

The boys were laughing as he encouraged them
to try a new trick, raising the ramp. They wouldn't
go first, so he grinned, skidded his bike round and
flew up the ramp. His bike landed with a thump
and he slid along the dirt with one foot down,
grinding to a halt a few metres from my window in
a shower of dust and grit. Holding on to the
handlebars, he turned back to his friends to shout
triumphantly at them in French, and then, facing
forwards again, he looked ahead and straight into
my eyes.

Wow! My heart did a double tuck and backflip
there and then. I thought I would never be able
to pull away from his melting stare, but then

someone gave a loud scream and broke the spell. Who was that? With open-the-ground-and-swallow-me-up horror, I realized it was me. Jack, conducting a rousing rendition of "The Wheels on the Bus" with his ice-cream cone, had dropped a large, freezing dollop of ice cream on to my bare legs. I frantically scrabbled around and tried to wipe it off with a handy wet-wipe. And when I looked up again dark-haired Bike Boy was gone.

Of course he was! I cursed myself for acting like such an idiot. That sort of thing would never, ever happen to Sasha – she's always in control of every situation. She would have had the nerve to smile at him and say something funny.

As I leaned back, I spotted my reflection in the rear-view mirror. Who was I kidding? A boy like that was never going to be interested in me anyway, with my olive-oily hair stuck to my pale no-time-for-fake-tan face. And if the fact I'd screamed like an idiot when he looked at me hadn't ruined my chances, I suspected the slight smell of sick that clung to me might have clinched it.

Mum and Dad returned, and we drove through the barrier into our new home. I stuffed the last of my ice-cream cone into my mouth and sighed; knowing my luck, Bike Boy was probably leaving that very day and I'd never see him again. But I really hoped he wasn't.

4

"I'm not going, you know I'm not going, you *know why* I'm not going and I cannot *believe* that you even imagined for one second that I'd go in the first place. You're driving me *mad*, Mum!" I was standing outside our tent with my towel and washbag under my arm.

"She didn't say you had to go," Dad said firmly. "And anyway, it's just *one* of the activities."

"Oh yes, like you weren't aware of it all along. No wonder you wouldn't let me see the brochure."

"Like I said, Amy, you don't have to go. It's totally

up to you. You can do all the other things and just leave that out; it's not a problem." Dad spread out a large map on the table and buried his head in it.

The morning had been almost pleasant until this conversation. The tent was surprisingly comfortable apart from an uninvited guest (I now had four unattractive mosquito bites adorning my left knee). I'd even managed to forget that I was sharing with a gently snoring five-year-old.

Mum folded up the brochure in a pointed fashion, and we set off for the showers in silence. And then I saw him. The dark-haired boy from the day before, cycling along ahead of us.

"What *are* you doing?" Mum gasped, as I ducked my head down and raised my towel over half my face. What was I *doing*? Did she really think I was going to risk anyone interesting seeing *me* first thing in the morning, with my untamed hair like a troll on the top of a pencil and a new little spot on my chin glinting away in the morning sunlight?

I watched as he disappeared round a corner, and then slipped into the refuge of the shower block.

So he was still around. I felt a tiny drop of hope. Could he be going to Teen Club? He was the right age. And there were French families staying on the campsite. Maybe I needed to revise my approach to Teen Club – after all there were lots of activities I *could* do… And there might be some OK people there…

As I was brushing my teeth, I noticed another girl, about my age, at the washbasins. She was very tall and very slim, with short, mousy hair, streaked with interesting orange patches. She had huge, curious, brown eyes, a long nose with a little bump in it and a wide, smiling mouth. She wasn't what you would call conventionally pretty, but there was something so alive about her that made her instantly appealing and interesting. She was complaining bitterly to her mother that she was NOT too young for professional highlights, as she tugged at her short crop and held up an orange streak to illustrate her pain.

"How am I ever going to get on in this world looking like an orang-utang? They do have hairdressers here, you know. No? Seriously, Mum?

You're saying no? Do they *have* Child Line in France?"

I smiled to myself. *She* seemed like fun.

When Mum and I got back, Dad had been to the campsite shop with Jack and returned with fresh croissants and baguettes. He had also made mugs of hot chocolate for Jack and me. I spread some pale French butter and strawberry jam on to the flaky croissant and thought that maybe, just maybe it wasn't going to be quite the hell I had imagined. (As long as I refused to acknowledge Dad's shorts.)

I gazed with mild curiosity at what Jack was spreading on his croissant, before asking, dead casually, "So, what other activities are there at Teen Club apart from … you know…"

Mum whipped out the brochure again.

"Mmm, now let me see – activities … oh, here we are … tennis, sailing…"

"Sailing! We're nowhere near the sea."

"No, but we are very near a beautiful lake … swimming…"

Now I had seen the pool on the campsite when we arrived and, although I obviously hadn't said so,

I was pretty impressed. It was huge – in fact there were two pools, one for young kids and a big one with slides and diving boards for everyone else.

Mum continued, "Cycling…" I looked up. Cycling? Cycling sounded *brilliant*. Maybe the dark-haired boy had got his bike from the club. Anyway, I stood more of a chance of bumping into him on a bike than a trampoline. Mum hesitated. "And, er … riding … but we've discussed that."

"Yes, we have."

"And you don't have to ride if you don't want to."

"I don't."

"That's fine, then."

"Yes, it is."

"I won't mention it again."

"Good."

And she folded up the brochure and we left it at that.

I had agreed to give Teen Club one day. And one day only. And if it was total rubbish that would be that. Me and Teen Club would go our separate ways. (Especially if Bike Boy and the interesting-looking girl weren't there, but obviously I hadn't

mentioned that bit.) Mum and Dad had sworn they would stick to this agreement.

Mum looked at her watch. "You need to leave in half an hour."

Half an hour! That was no time to get ready. A serious effort was called for, but a serious effort that obviously looked like no effort had been made at all. I had managed to wash the last of the oil out and blow-dry my troll-like hair into submission at the showers, but now I had to decide what to wear and put on some make-up. I had to improve on the hot, greasy, sick-smelling girl Bike Boy had first seen in the car.

I retreated into the tent. Things were not helped by my lack of mirror. I bribed Jack with the promise of a story to hold up my make-up compact, which had a mirror in the lid, but his arms kept getting tired and drooping.

First I tried on a denim skirt, good for showing off my legs, which, though pale, were smooth and one of my better points. Jack held the mirror at exhausted ankle level. I shook my head and wriggled out of it.

"What are you doin'?" Jack wailed. "My arms are fallin' off me."

"Skirts aren't so good for trampolining or cycling," I said.

"Why?"

"Amy doesn't want everyone to see her pants," Mum explained, coming in to tidy up Jack's bed.

"*Mum!*" I shrieked.

But it was too late; Jack had gone into that snuffly, snorty, giggly mode he always does when someone has said something unbearably funny. So amused was he that he fell off the camp bed and continued sniggering on the floor. Mum and I ignored him.

"Are you going to wear that halter-neck?" Mum asked, looking at me in that special way she does.

"Why? What's wrong with it?"

"It's just that the activities might be quite, er … active and you can't really wear a bra with that top, can you? I mean I know you're not exactly huge, but…"

"*Mum!*"

The word "bra" set Jack off again. "Bras are for

Amy

your bezzooms." He pulled his sleeping bag over his head. "Your bezzooms are in your bra…" The sleeping bag shook silently.

"Shut up, Jack. It's not funny and you're being very silly. Thanks very much, Mum, I've lost my mirror now." I bent down and picked it up from the floor where Jack had dropped it.

"Here, I'll hold it for you."

"Thanks, but no. I've got a better idea. Why don't you both go away and let me get dressed in private."

"OK, OK, but I don't know what was wrong with the white T-shirt and blue shorts you were wearing earlier. You looked very pretty." Mum sighed and leaned over to pick up Jack, who was now clutching his tummy and complaining that he wasn't feeling very well.

After another fifteen minutes of trying things on and throwing them off, holding the mirror at arm's length and scanning my body in a 10cm square, I had to agree with her – the shorts and T-shirt worked best.

Finally, I looked at my face. Hair now tamed with

conditioner, a dab of concealer on the spot, a layer of suncream and a lick of waterproof mascara. All I needed now was a bit of lipstick. Mum is funny about lipstick, but we compromised on tinted lipsalves. I opened my new strawberry-flavoured one. It was empty. I dashed outside the tent to check in my purse. Jack was spitting something pink into a tissue Mum was holding for him.

"He put it on his croissant, didn't he?"

Jack's chest gave an indignant heave. "You shouldn't put pictures of strawberries on things you can't eat. It's not nice."

I opened my mouth.

Mum held up her hand. "I'll buy you another one," she soothed. "Now you'd better get going. You know where you've got to meet everyone, don't you? I showed you last night. Or do you want me to come along with you, seeing as it's your first day?"

Lipsalve or no lipsalve, I was out of there in a flash.

5

My pace slowed down as I approached the clubhouse. It was one thing to dash away from Mum's insane suggestion that she accompany me there, it was quite another to walk up to a bunch of total strangers that might include Bike Boy. I began to envy Jack's world, where a tramp-amp-poline was all that was necessary for everlasting bliss and it never occurred to you to worry about what other people thought. But I did care what other people thought — all of my friends were the same; even Sasha, who seemed not to care, did a bit.

I had now slowed down to what could only be described as a standstill. The image of Bike Boy floated in front of me, but as I stood there it morphed into Ralph Levinson... I sighed – let's face it, which was the more likely?

My thoughts were interrupted by the sound of a girl's voice. "Mum! I swear if you take one step further I will die! No, not die – run away, run away in France and you won't see me again for years and years. I'll be found starving in an attic in Paris. *And it'll be too late to save me!*" I looked round – the voice was coming from behind a row of tents.

"*You took another step!* Not one more step, I said. I will not go to this stupid club if you... What! I-don't-believe-it-you-took-another-step! Do I have to beat you back with a stick? I *know* where to go."

The tall girl from the washbasins rounded the corner, followed doggedly by her smaller, but very determined, mother.

"It's not that I want to go with you to the club, Lily," she sighed. "I don't, but we both know that you can't find your way to the bottom of the

garden, let alone around the campsite, where all the rows of tents look so similar. Sense of direction is not your strong point..."

"I know exactly where I am," the girl said firmly, with her hands on her hips. "And if you keep following me, I'm not going at all."

Her mother sighed. "So you *absolutely* know where the clubhouse is?"

"I do."

"Definitely?"

"Definitely."

"I could take you a bit nearer..."

"No! I know where it is. I really, truly do."

"It's by the—"

"I know, Mum."

"Well, if you're sure."

"I am."

"Well, OK then."

"OK, bye!"

"Bye."

At that, the woman disappeared back down the row of tents they had come from.

"Au revoir, Maman." The girl gave her mother a

dramatic wave.

She then looked calmly up and down the road before purposefully striding off. In the wrong direction.

"Hey!" I found myself shouting. "Hey!"

She turned round, gave me a questioning look, then smiled.

"Hey to you, too. What's up?"

"Erm … you're, um … sort of going in the wrong direction for the clubhouse." I felt myself blush.

"Oh no, am I?" She began to laugh. "I'm so hopeless, I lose myself in my own bedroom sometimes… It all looks the same here, doesn't it? It's like a maze."

She looked at me again. "Do you know where it is, then? This clubhouse all teen life is supposed to be heading towards, like the Children of the Damned…"

She raised her arms in front of her and began to stagger along the path, zombie style.

"Er … still the wrong direction," I said hesitantly.

She swerved around 180 degrees and came alongside me. "Well," she said, dropping her arms,

"I wasn't expecting to meet someone before I actually got there. That's a bit lucky; shall we pretend that we've known each other all our lives and intimidate everyone else who will be feeling nervous and self-conscious by laughing smugly and whispering a lot?"

I looked at her, surprised. She didn't seem that kind of girl at all. She grinned at my puzzled face.

"It's just that's what they're doing." She indicated two girls ahead of us on the path. Sure enough, the fair-haired girl's ponytail swung round and she gave us a cool stare, before turning back to whisper something to her even blonder companion.

The tall girl raised her eyebrows at me. "See what I mean?" We were now standing outside the clubhouse door that the fair-haired girl and her friend had just let go in our faces. "Well, come on, let's get it over with then. I'm Lily, by the way; who are you?"

"Amy."

"Amy. Nice name. I don't mind mine, but I'm not sure if I'm going to keep my surname."

"What, when you get married?"

"What? No! When I'm an actress. Lily Pocklehurst just isn't going to sound right. What do you think? I just can't decide. I suppose it might get me the part of a maid in some old-fashioned drama. Do you think I should have a nose job? Be *absolutely* honest…"

But before I could answer, a large, blonde Australian girl of about nineteen coughed loudly and introduced herself as "Pit", though her badge said "Pat". She ticked our names off on a clipboard and showed us the bike rack. We were all going to be allocated a bike for our own use around the campsite as well as for organized rides.

"Fantastic!" I couldn't help saying.

Lily looked at me strangely. I blushed. "Well, you never know who you might meet," I added shyly.

She arched her eyebrows. "Indeed, Miss Dark Horse. Could I be right in thinking that you may have already spotted that special someone?"

"No!"

"Well, I hope you're lying," she sighed, "because from the look of it, it's slim pickings round here…"

Amy

And indeed I felt a rush of disappointment scanning the gang of teenagers milling around the clubhouse, for nowhere among them was the face that I had been so desperately hoping to see.

"Is he here?" I turned around, startled. It was the girl with the ponytail talking. Could she read my mind?

"Don't think so," her friend replied.

"Typical." Ponytail Girl sighed dramatically. "The only boy I've spotted who I might possibly want to get to know on this whole campsite and he's not here." She tossed her sleek hair back, and screwed up her perfect little nose. "Never mind. I'm bound to come across him soon, and when I do he's going to get the full Vicky treatment. Remember what to look out for: a tall, dark, handsome French boy with gorgeous eyes…"

6

"Hey, Amy, what's up! You're in a daze there, come on!" Pit's voice broke into my whirling thoughts as I processed what Vicky had just said. With an effort I managed a smile and joined the others.

When Pit decided that there were enough ticks on her clipboard, she began to herd us like wayward sheep into a reluctant huddle at one end of the clubhouse.

"Hi, everyone, great to see you," she yelled heartily.

There was a subdued murmur in response.

Amy

"C'mon now, guys, you can do better than that! Let's do some proper introductions, names first."

Everyone looked at each other. It was obvious that the members of Teen Club had already formed distinct groups. Pit began with the French teens: four elegant, sleek-haired girls of about sixteen years old and three stocky boys. Even though the girls were in shorts and T-shirts like me, they were the neatest, chicest shorts and T-shirts that I had ever seen. As they stood there, perfectly groomed, and introduced themselves in their great accents, you could only look on and admire. The French boys were younger than me. Sadly for them, you could tell their enthusiastic efforts to impress the girls were doomed.

Pit moved on to the three tall, friendly Dutch girls and two equally towering German boys. They were also all older than us, and you could see the bonding going on with *them* already.

Then it was our turn. In our English group we were all more or less the same age. I now had reason to pay special attention to Vicky, the girl with the ponytail. She was taller than me, with

long, golden limbs, spotless white shorts and a tight, pink T-shirt. With her heart-shaped face, large brown eyes and clear skin she was gorgeous and she knew it.

As she chatted to her friend, who I now knew was called Selina, she continuously cast her eyes around the clubhouse to see who was watching. Most of the boys had noticed her, especially the two boys who had prompted Lily's observation on the talent earlier.

They turned out to be twins called Tom and Jed. There was also an attractive, smiley girl, Diane, and a tall, gangly boy. He stood next to us, taller than Lily, with dark-blond hair that stuck out at odd angles. He kept his eyes on the ground, obviously feeling very self-conscious.

"Greg," he murmured when it was his turn. Vicky sniggered and whispered something to Selina. Greg flushed.

I glared at them. I hate it when people think it's funny to make people feel uncomfortable on purpose. Lily must have felt the same way because when Pit told us to get on our bikes for our tour of

the area we both fell on him at the same time and said hello with such enthusiasm the poor boy was quite overwhelmed.

"You friends?" he asked, as we bowled along past the tennis court, with Pit giving a running commentary in front.

Lily and I looked at each other.

"Well," I began, but whatever I was going to say was drowned out by the bells of Vicky and Selina's bikes as they overtook us.

"Dump, isn't it?" Vicky commented as they passed. "And not a decent boy in sight either."

"Hey, watch what you're saying. We might be feeling the same way about you *girls*, you know." It was Tom and Jed, their faces already red from the exertion of the ride, for if the truth be told they weren't exactly what you'd call fit.

Vicky threw her head back and laughed, showing her perfect cheerleader teeth. "Yeah, sure," she said, and then lost interest because she needed to pedal frantically to get to the front so she could tell Pit how brilliant she was at tennis.

"But it's not my best thing," we heard her say.

"My best thing is riding."

"*Eeeueww.* '*My best thing is riding.*'" Lily mimicked accurately, but I couldn't even pretend to smile. My heart began to beat faster and my hands began to feel sweaty on the handlebars. I had to speak to Pit, to tell her that I wasn't doing any riding. But it would be too public to talk to her now; everyone would hear. I'd do it at the end of the day, when the others had gone.

"You all right, Amy?" Lily asked, pedalling along beside me.

I nodded, but we were now cycling out of the campsite and along the road I had come down in the car when I arrived. On a sharp corner there was a sign with a horse's head on it.

"Oh, here we go – the stables," Lily laughed. "Have you ever ridden before?"

I didn't reply. She looked curiously at me.

"You know there's nothing to be scared of, I'm sure. I've never been on a horse in my life. I'll be terrified, but I bet it will be fun, too, you'll see. Anyway, we're not riding today, we're just on a tour of our new surroundings." She nudged me

Amy

with her elbow; my bike wobbled. "You sure you're all right?" Lily was frowning, looking anxiously at me now.

"Sure," I replied huskily, as I stared up at the stable yard entrance.

We got off our bikes and leaned them up against the wall. I looked for Pit, but she had already disappeared through the archway into the yard. I hung back, pretending to check my bike for an imaginary puncture, but Tom and Lily came over and offered to help.

"Come on, Amy, your tyre is fine. Let's get moving," Tom laughed.

Taking a deep breath, I walked into the yard, staying close to the reassuring figure of Lily. The sights and smells overwhelmed me: a horse leaning lazily out of its stall, shaking the flies off from time to time; the dark recesses of the tack room in the corner; and the messy office, papered with Post-its and scrappy notes. It was all so familiar to me and yet all so strange. Pit was in the office, talking in French to an attractive woman with dark-brown hair tied back in a scarf.

I couldn't believe that I'd made it this far. My head was spinning and my hands were clammy. Every bit of me wanted to run away. All around me people were bustling about, relaxed and cheerful. What would they think if I suddenly bolted? I couldn't. I had to leave without making a fuss. Or a fool of myself. A wave of nausea rose up in my throat. I couldn't be sick. That would be the worst thing I could do. I reached out my hand to steady myself against the wall. I *had* to find a way to escape.

"Crap horses," Vicky sneered loudly, "and dump of a stable, absolute dump. When they said 'riding' in the activities I was hoping for something on a more professional scale than this."

The Frenchwoman stopped talking and gave Vicky a level stare. I had a feeling she had understood every word.

"I think they look amazing," Lily gasped, as a huge grey was led out by a stable girl into the middle of the yard. It was the closest I had been to a horse for a very long time. I could feel my breath quicken and my heart tighten with fear. I pressed

my back into the wall and felt a trickle of sweat run down my forehead.

But in spite of my terror, I could still see that Lily was right and Vicky was wrong. The horses in this stable were in wonderful condition – they may not have been thoroughbreds, but they were good quality animals. And I was thinking to myself that at least I could do that; at least I could appreciate the beauty of horses even though I didn't like this one being so close to me. If I could just hold on, we'd be out of here soon and then I could talk to Pit at the end of the day and tell her I wouldn't be doing any riding.

"Pit says that we can fill up the water buckets and put them in the empty stalls," Lily beamed. She was already opening the half door of a stall, carrying an overflowing bucket in her other hand. "She says there's a ride due back any minute and the horses will be thirsty."

"You must be joking!" Vicky sneered. "Getting us to do their dirty work in the stables? Forget it."

"Well, I saw it more like caring for tired, hot animals, but there you go," Lily responded sharply.

Secretly, I was glad to have something to do. *"You can do this,"* I said to myself. I grabbed a bucket and put it under the gushing tap by the tack room. As soon as it was full, I gripped the handle tightly and searched for a refuge. If I could just find an empty stall and get out of the yard, I could hide away until it was time to go.

I found what I was looking for and slipped inside, away from the towering presence of the grey in the yard. I leaned against the far wall, adjusted my eyes to the shadowy light and told myself again that if I stayed there and waited till Pit called us all to go, I would be able to survive the experience without making a total fool of myself. I heard Lily ask Tom and Jed where I was. A minute later, the loud clatter of hooves on the warm flagstones told me the ride had returned.

My heart started to beat faster; outside were at least six or seven horses, all milling about, snorting and stamping, powerful and heavy. I began to panic. If I stayed where I was, I would be trapped if anyone came in, and in a very small space. I had to get out.

Amy

I took a step forward, but I was too late, the door swung open and a fresh-faced young woman led a large bay straight at me. I let out a gasp and the woman looked up, surprised. I indicated with a nod of my head the bucket, now clutched in both my hands, and she nodded and smiled. She gestured for me to put the bucket down, but I couldn't move. I was paralyzed with fear, and the horse, thirsty after a long ride in the hot sun, smelled the water and came straight at me, pushing its long neck against me as it nuzzled for the bucket.

"Please," I begged. I could hardly speak. "Get it away from me, please."

The horse, frustrated by not getting the drink it wanted so badly, suddenly threw up its massive head and gave it a tremendous shake. I dropped the bucket on to the straw and he started back, ears flattened. I waved my arms in front of my face. "Get him away from me! Please! Please! Go away! Go away!"

The woman was staring at me, confused. The horse shied back a little and a hoof hit the bucket with a clatter, which caused him to shy again.

The woman grasped his halter and held him firmly, but by this time I'd lost it. "Get him away! Get him away!" I shouted, whilst inside I was saying, "*No no no*, stop making a fool of yourself, you idiot." But I couldn't stop myself crying out. Even though the horse was standing calmly now, I just couldn't keep the fear in. Pit and the Frenchwoman appeared and I could hear Pit talking to me, but I couldn't make sense of it.

The woman quickly tied the horse up, then gently but firmly took my arm, lifting me from the straw where I was crouching. Keeping herself between me and the horse, she led me out into the bright sunshine of the stable yard, where the whole of Teen Club stood in a semicircle, open-mouthed. Staring.

"What *was* all that about?" Vicky gasped. "I've heard of being scared of horses, but honestly, Amy … that was way over the top."

"That's enough, Vicky," Pit said in a warning tone. "Are you OK, Amy? You're not hurt at all?"

I shook my head, but I felt an overwhelming desire to cry. I bit my lip hard. There was a

moment of embarrassed silence. "Come on then, let's get out of the sun." Pit led me away from all the staring eyes into the office, where the nice Frenchwoman handed me a glass of water.

"Are you OK now?" Pit asked anxiously. "Have you always been so scared of horses? You should've said before and I wouldn't have brought you here."

"I was going to say that I didn't want to ride, it was just…"

I looked out at the gang of teens now sitting on the ground, leaning with their backs against the wall in the sunshine … waiting.

Pit followed my gaze. "I can understand that you didn't want to say anything in front of a bunch of guys you've only just met, but I wish you'd said something to *me*. I'm supposed to be looking after you, and look at you! Do you want me to lose my job?" she joked.

I managed a weak smile. "Sorry."

Pit smiled back. "We're going to cycle to the lake now; there's a picnic arranged. It'll be a chance to relax a bit and get over, um … your fright."

But any feelings of fear I may have had were now taken over by new, equally strong, emotions — shame and humiliation. I knew my face was burning. "If you don't mind, I think I'll go back to the camp now. I know the way back on my bike."

Pit looked disappointed.

"It's just that I'm not actually feeling that well," I continued. "I think I'll go back and have a lie-down."

"Hey, don't do that — come with us, you can't leave me here all on my own."

It was Lily, who was leaning precariously over the half door of the office. I couldn't help giving her a watery smile, but then I heard the sound of Vicky's braying laughter ringing around the yard.

I felt a hot wave of embarrassment and looked away. Lily must think I was a total idiot. I was leaving her at the stables and I could tell she didn't really understand why. I wanted to be her friend so much, she was great, but I *couldn't* stay here with the others. Not after what had happened. She probably thought I was a wimp anyway, and you could add pathetic and hysterical to that, too.

"No thanks," I said curtly. "I'm not feeling very well; I want to go back."

I saw a shadow of hurt cross Lily's face. "OK, if that's what you want."

"It is," I said, and she withdrew from the door without another word.

I got up slowly and dusted the straw off my shorts. I said thank you to the Frenchwoman and Pit, before Pit walked me through the yard, over to my bike.

Brilliant, I thought as I pedalled furiously back towards the campsite, *now Lily won't want to be my friend*. Not that I could blame her after my weird behaviour. Although Pit told the others that I was going home because I wasn't feeling well, the sidelong glances on that walk from the office back to my bike told me no one believed the story. I knew one thing for certain. I wasn't going back to Teen Club.

7

"Why, Amy, what on earth's the matter?"

I got back to our tent and wordlessly threw my bike on the ground. I ran inside and flung myself on to my camp bed – I didn't want to talk to anyone, least of all Mum. Luckily, one of the good things about her is that she sometimes knows when to leave me alone.

After a while, Dad came to the entrance of my sleeping compartment and passed me a glass of orange juice. "You OK, Amy?" he enquired gently. "Feeling better?" I wasn't, but I nodded.

"Well, as you're here, would you like to take Jack to the pool? Mum and I wouldn't mind having a stroll, but Jack's desperate to go swimming. You'd be doing us a big favour if you could…"

"I'll do it," I said. At least I'd make someone happy and it gave me a reason to get out of the boring, stuffy tent.

"Are you sad, Amy?" Jack asked as we got into the baby pool. He brought his face up close and stared at me intently.

"A bit." I sighed, pausing from blowing up his armbands.

"Is it because you don't like your club?"

"Mmm, sort of…"

"You can join mine," he said brightly. "We have juice and biscuits."

"That sounds great, Jack, but I don't think I want to be in any club."

"But then you'll be all on your own. Please join my club. They don't mind about pants. Everyone shows their pants on our tramp-amp-poline." He tried again, "Or about bras."

I couldn't stop myself smiling as I threaded his

arms into the Scooby Doo armbands.

"Well, I'm glad to hear it."

"You could help me be friends with Hélène, too."

"Really, Jack? How could I do that?"

"She likes swimming."

"Does she? Well, that's nice."

"She can swim without armbands." He reached out to grab his inflatable rubber ring with a crocodile head on the front, which was drifting off.

"Well, *she's* very clever, isn't she?"

"Yes, she is very clever, but she says I'm too splashy and she doesn't like it when I do this."

Jack began to beat the water with his arms in that frenzied manner that he firmly calls "swimming". He sat up again. "She says, 'Non, non, allay, allay!' And 'allay' means 'go away', you know, which isn't a very nice thing to say really…" His expression drooped. Hélène must be a very tough cookie indeed to resist that face.

"You just need some more practice and then you won't need armbands or, um … this." I grabbed his crocodile ring and, to cheer him up, plonked it on my head.

"There's a splashy, dangerous crocodile coming to get you in the shallows..." I growled, before plunging underwater and crawling along the bottom towards his little kicking legs. I could hear him shrieking with delight as I followed his now escaping bottom half through the pool. I emerged, pulling the crocodile more firmly down on my tangled hair, to face Jack's laughter at the edge of the pool.

"You've got hair all over your face! You are the crocodile monster!" he cheered. I parted my dripping locks and looked up... At two tanned legs in a pair of faded navy shorts. I pulled the last of the wet strands out of my eyes and found myself gazing straight into the face of Bike Boy.

He was standing holding a towel under his arm, and he was staring right at me. His large, grey eyes were fringed with the longest, blackest lashes I had ever seen. It would have been the most romantic moment ever, if I hadn't been sitting in less than a foot of water with a plastic crocodile on my head. Without taking his eyes away from mine, his face broke into a dazzling, heart-stopping smile.

"Jean Paul! Allez!" Two of his friends were calling. He turned, and then looked back with a final grin, before slowly following them over to the big pool.

I gazed after him. *Terrific.* The most gorgeous boy in the world reappears in my life and I'm doing an impersonation of the witch in *The Little Mermaid.* Still, at least I knew his name now. "Jean Paul. Jean Paul." I began to silently repeat it over and over as I lifted the crocodile from my bedraggled head.

"Was that your friend?" Jack asked, taking the ring from me and attempting to climb into it.

"No, it wasn't," I replied. "I don't know who he is." I shook my head at Jack and showered him with drops of water.

"Feeling better, then?" I looked up. It was Vicky, with Selina, Diane and the twins; the club must've finished for the day. I peered behind them, but there was no sign of Lily. "Interesting look," Vicky giggled.

"Coming swimming?" Diane interrupted.

"Looks like Amy's got her hands full," Vicky said.

Amy

"Are you babysitting your little brother?"

I nodded. Vicky had a way of making you feel very small.

"Well, come later if you can," Diane smiled.

Vicky rolled her eyes, but then gave me a tight smile. "Yeah, come and join us later – if you can." And suddenly she reminded me of Sasha, how she speaks to Polly sometimes, but I pushed the thought out of my mind. Sasha was my friend; Vicky certainly wasn't.

"Er … yes. OK." I didn't want to go anywhere with the Teen Club crowd after this morning. But they were heading for the pool where Jean Paul was hanging out with his mates. Vicky was bound to spot him, and with her super-pretty looks and confidence I knew if she got to speak to him first, any dreams I had would be over. But even if I wanted to join them, I couldn't. I had to look after Jack.

"*Go on!* Go, Amy. I'm here now. I'll stay with Jack. You go and have a proper swim in the big pool…" Mum had arrived, successfully merging hideous timing with being the most embarrassing

parent in the world. I flushed a deep red. There was an awkward silence. I saw Vicky look round at the others, but I couldn't see her expression.

"Er ... it's OK, I don't mind staying."

"Nonsense!" Mum cried cheerily. "You go and have a good time."

Then everyone waited in more silence, as you do when someone's Mum is around, until, defeated by the whole situation, I felt there was nothing for me to do but climb out of the baby pool and wander over with them.

No one said anything about what had happened at the stables. In fact, no one had time to say anything because as soon as we neared the dark blue of the deep end, something attracted Vicky's attention: Jean Paul climbing out of the water at the far end. Any hopes I may have had that he wasn't the boy she was talking about this morning were dispelled in an instant.

"Oh my God!" She grabbed Selina's arm. "Do my eyes deceive me or is that the boy I was talking about yesterday? Isn't he gorgeous?" She laughed as she made a beeline for where Jean Paul now

sat, drying his hair roughly and talking to his friends. "Come on, Selina!"

I was so clearly not involved in this invitation that I wasn't quite sure what to do next: follow them and have Jean Paul think I was some sad "hanger on", go back to Mum and Jack, or just disappear. I decided on the last option. I dived into the cool water and started swimming in the very opposite direction that my heart wanted me to go in.

As I finished the length and was swimming back, I saw that Vicky hadn't wasted a moment. She was now sitting between Jean Paul and his friend on the edge of the pool, splashing them with her long brown legs and doing a lot of blonde hair swishing, while Selina and the twins sat watchfully nearby.

Diane had decided to swim as well. She smiled as she passed me. I looked up. Vicky was talking away, twirling her hair and swinging her legs. Her expensive, white bikini fitted her perfectly and looked fabulous. Even without a crocodile on my head, I knew I wasn't looking my best. But as I drew nearer I thought there was no harm in just saying hello.

Vicky saw me first. "Look everyone! It's the Crocodile Ness Monster! Save me, save me!" She began to kick her slim legs frantically to and fro. I was glad of the churning water as, although I pretended to laugh, I felt a bit stupid and confused. I couldn't look at Jean Paul. I couldn't imagine *what* he was thinking. I decided to just carry on swimming and smiling.

"Help me!" Vicky cried, and threw her arms around Jean Paul. Tom and Jed, desperate to impress her and not at all happy to see this new development with the unknown French boy, took matters into their own hands.

"I'll save you, Vicky!" Tom cried, doing a bomb into the water. He jumped to one side of me, but the waves knocked me sideways. "How was that?" he shouted.

"Didn't work!" Vicky replied, clinging on to Jean Paul's arm. "I know," she called out loudly to Jed, as he was lining up to take a running jump. "Try neighing and swishing your tail a bit... That should do it!"

"Shhh, don't be mean!" I heard Diane hiss

sharply, as she swam up behind me, but it was too late. I had heard. My fake smile disappeared and tears sprang into my eyes. I couldn't let Vicky see that I cared. I turned and began to swim furiously away.

"Oh come on, Amy," I heard Vicky cry. "Sense of humour failure or what? I was only joking!"

"It's not that, I'm fine. Just got to go now!" I yelled in as normal a voice as I could manage. But I was seething. She wasn't joking at all. And she was bound to tell Jean Paul about what had happened at the stable, to explain what the "joke" had been all about.

As I plunged through the water, I wondered if he was sitting on the edge of the pool laughing about me with Vicky. *Well, let him*, I thought angrily. *If he's the sort of boy that thinks that kind of thing is a joke, she's welcome to him. I bet they're both having a big laugh about Miss Scaredy-pants Crocodile Head.* But, all the same, I couldn't bear to look round to see if it was true.

After a morning of supreme boredom reading Mum's chick lit, I was so desperate to do something I volunteered to take Jack to the pool again. Teen Club wasn't over for a few hours so I was safe from more of Vicky's "jokes". As I waded into the baby pool, I told myself off for being disappointed that *he* wasn't there, and concentrated on shouting encouragement to a madly-kicking Jack, who was holding on to a float for dear life. I was unsuccessfully trying to teach him the fundamental rule of swimming: that action

needs to take place at the back end as well as the front, otherwise serious sinking inevitably occurs.

I was so engrossed in this task that I didn't notice I was being watched at first.

A quiet cough made me look up. Lily lowered herself gingerly into the water next to us. Her tiny, yellow bikini made her look taller and thinner than ever. Her hands flew up in front of her chest.

"Don't look at me in this!" she shrieked. "I told my mum I needed a spray-on St Tropez tan before we came out, but would she listen?" She raised her hands again, but this time to protect herself from Jack's splashing. "Could you turn him down a bit?" she frowned. Jack, tired out by now, was glad to have a chance to rest, and headed to the steps where some other children were playing.

"You weren't at Teen Club today," Lily observed.

"Well, after yesterday I didn't feel—"

"Yesterday, smesh-terday, that's what I say," she interrupted. "Something happened that frightened you in the stable and you got upset. No big deal."

"No big deal! I'm glad you think it was no big deal. I made a total idiot of myself! I only had to

69

look at your faces when I came out. Every one of you was staring at me as if I was a lunatic."

Lily flushed. "I'm so sorry about that, Amy. The last thing I wanted was to make you feel bad. You're the nicest person on the whole campsite. It's just that I didn't know what was going on. I did *try* to talk to you later, you know." I blushed, remembering how I had responded. "It was kind of a shock the, er … screaming. We thought something terrible had happened."

I looked down. "Well, in a kind of way, I thought it had…"

Lily looked at me, puzzled.

I took a deep breath. "I thought I was going to … get hurt. I know that sounds mad to you, but I'm terrified of horses, really terrified."

"But *why*?"

"Because I did, once … get hurt." I couldn't believe I was opening up to someone I'd only just met, but it felt OK.

Lily's eyes widened. "Riding?"

I nodded.

"What happened?"

And so I sat in the pool and told her about the accident and how I'd been in hospital for a while, and afterwards she whistled and said, "Phew! No wonder you're a bit nervous around horses, then. But you do know that that was just a one-off, an accident?"

"I know, I know, but I can't help it. I just can't go near them again. I know it's hard to understand…"

"I can a tiny bit."

"What do you mean?"

"Well, I know what it's like to want to avoid something and to spend a great deal of effort doing so."

"Now what are *you* talking about?"

"Ask me why I'm not at Teen Club."

"Oh yes, you're not, are you? Why aren't you at Teen Club, Lily?"

"Because they're at the lake."

"And that would be a problem why?"

"Promise you won't laugh."

"Cross my heart and hope to die."

"I can't swim. It's a sure sign of how desperate I am to seek you out that I'm in this baby pool at all."

"You didn't have a terrible swimming accident and nearly drown, did you? Because that would be just freaky."

"Naaah!" she grinned. "Nothing so dramatic, simply never got round to learning," she sighed.

"I know I'm going to have to go back to the club, but I just couldn't quite face the smug friends without you. Me and Greg and Diane miss you. They're good fun; I like them a lot. Which reminds me, who's the boy you want to find on your bike?"

"No one," I blushed.

Lily laughed. "You're the worst liar in a world championship 'worst liars' competition, Amy. Come on, spill…"

I took a deep breath and then exhaled my words in a rush. "Well, he's called Jean Paul; he cycles around the campsite, but doesn't go to Teen Club. He's absolutely gorgeous, but…" I had to stop for breath.

"But?"

"Vicky fancies him and she's met him now. I tried to get to speak to him at the pool yesterday, but she made a joke about the stable thing and I'm

sure she's told him all about it. And anyway, it's totally hopeless as she's so pretty. I haven't a chance, so I'm just going to GIVE UP."

Lily's nostrils flared slightly. She pushed a child floating too close gently away. "I see. Frankly, Amy, I'll be honest with you – I'm just a little disappointed."

"What?"

"You haven't even spoken to him yet!"

I shrugged my shoulders.

"Talking is a good start. And anyway, you're miles prettier than Vicky."

"No I'm not."

"OK, no you're not. I'm lying. You are bus-stoppingly plain, and in fact I'm off now to get a paper bag for you to put over your head. I can lead you around the campsite for the rest of the holidays. Don't worry, I'll draw a really beautiful face on the bag; no one will ever know the hideousness that lurks inside…"

I began to laugh.

"That's better. Don't you realize that it's because you're so pretty that Vicky is mean to you?

73

She's jealous of anyone more attractive than her and wants them out of her way. She wants to be Queen Bee. But we're not going to let her succeed. You and me, we're going to track down this heart-throb Jean Paul who's causing all this commotion, and you are NOT going to GIVE UP. OK? What do they say? It's not over till the fat lady sings … and what about the disco?"

"What disco?"

"Haven't you read the brochure?"

"Er, not really."

"Well, there's a disco type thing for the Teen Club. Where love blooms – so I'm told. That's why Vicky's got her eye on this French boy. She wants to go with him."

"Well, she will then, won't she?"

"HAVE YOU NOT BEEN LISTENING TO A WORD I'VE SAID?" Lily yelled. "Change the attitude, Cinderella. Don't let those ugly sister, smug friends bother you."

"Not at all ugly though, are they?" I moped.

Lily looked at me and sighed. "Let's try and be positive now, Amy. I've told you why Vicky's like

she is with you. Now promise me you won't give up. You've got me now."

"You're good at sorting out other people, aren't you?" I smiled.

Out of the corner of my eye I saw Jack drifting past, lying on his float and smiling dreamily.

"I could teach you, Lily."

"Teach me what?"

"Teach you to swim. I'm teaching Jack; you could just join our lessons. You could come after Teen Club. Vicky need never know… We could pretend we were both teaching him, that you were *demonstrating*…"

"Oh, I don't really care about what she thinks." Lily ran her fingers through her short hair. "She'd get bored of teasing me soon enough, and move on to someone else. *However*…" She gave me a long, hard stare.

"Stop looking at me like that, you're making me nervous."

"Let's help each other out. I'll agree to you teaching me to swim, if you'll agree not to give up on French Boy. And to come back to Teen Club."

She watched my face. "*Pleeeease*. I'm begging you here. The smug friends and the twins aren't interested in me, they think I'm weird, the nice Dutch girls only want to flirt with the German boys and the French girls are all so scary and sort of … neat. They just don't get me. You're the only one who really gets me. Go on, go on, go on." She took a deep breath and continued, "*Go on, go on, go on…*"

"OK! OK!" I yelled, putting my hands over my ears.

"She *shall* go to the ball!" Lily cheered. "We begin 'Operation French Boy' forthwith!"

She leaped up and dragged me with her. And at least three small children in rubber rings were sent eddying to the poolside.

9

"I'll have to take Jack to the pool a bit later today."

Dad stopped reading and peered over his paper. "Mmm. Exciting plans?"

"I'm, er ... going to give Teen Club another try."

"Amy, that's great!" Mum cried. "I *told* you you'd make friends and..."

Dad shot her a warning look.

"And, well, that's just *fine*, isn't it? Fine with us?" She looked at Dad. He winked at me and nodded.

Mum looked at her watch. "Don't you think you'd better be heading off, then?"

"I will be in a minute. I'm waiting for a friend. We're going together."

Mum opened her mouth to say something else, but Dad gave his newspaper a little shake and she shut it again.

"Is your friend the long girl with orange hair who tipped everyone over in the pool?"

"She is. And Jack, her name is Lily."

"Well, Lily's comin' up the road."

"Your mum and dad look nice," Lily said as we headed for the clubhouse. She paused to glance at a poster on a tree advertising a visiting funfair.

"What? Well, yes, I suppose they are. Mum's a bit anxious, though. About me. Sometimes."

"Tell me about it! You're lucky. It's only me and my mum. I haven't got a brother to share the spotlight of her undivided attention. My dad left when I was little, and I hardly ever see him as he's so far away. He lives in America and he's a cameraman. Which is so cool, don't you think? Wouldn't it just be the weirdest thing if one day

he was a cameraman on a movie that I was starring in?"

As we walked on to the clubhouse, I suddenly felt overwhelmed with anxiety. What if everyone just stood and stared at me again, like at the stables, or worse, if they whispered and sneered?

"Do you know if Vicky is coming today?" I asked.

Lily put her hands on her hips. "*Amy!* I'm sharing my innermost hopes and dreams with you and all you are thinking about is the opinion of a silly girl with a ponytail, who, and I'm being quite honest here, obviously doesn't give a *hoot* about what *you* think about *her*," Lily sighed. "Frankly," she looked away with a sniff, "I'm rather hurt."

I couldn't help breaking into a smile, and as I did so she gave me a shove in the back and propelled me through the door.

There was no sign of Vicky or Selina.

"Amy! Great to see you." It was Pit; she looked up from her clipboard and gave me a huge smile.

"Hi, Amy!" Diane grinned and gave me a thumbs up. Greg waved a long, slender hand in my general direction and nodded his head.

Tom and Jed, after a flurry of furious conversation between themselves, shuffled over.

"Er … um … hi, Amy," Jed murmured, blushing. "Glad you came back. Sorry about the pool thing."

"We didn't mean… You know, we were just messing about…"

"It's OK."

They both looked hugely relieved and grinned broadly. "You've got to come to the lake, you know, it's awesome," Tom urged.

"Totally," Jed agreed.

I took a deep breath. It was going to be OK.

"Gather round, gather round," Pit clucked. "I need to tell you what we're doing today."

She looked up. "Where's Vicky and Selina?"

The door banged shut. "Sorry we're late." Vicky's gaze roamed around the room. When she saw me, she stopped dead. She raised her eyebrows, but said nothing.

"Right, let's get on with the activities of the day," Pit paused briefly, "now that we're all here."

"I can hardly wait," Vicky drawled. Pit shot her a frosty look over her clipboard.

"Today it's beach volleyball. It doesn't matter if you don't know how to play, it's easy to pick up, and you can cool off in the lake afterwards. So let's get going and not waste any more of this glorious sunshine. The minibus is outside."

"*Beach* volleyball?" Lily and I chorused together.

"Yes," Vicky replied, "*beach* volleyball. You know, the sandy stuff. You see, if either of you had actually *been* with us on the lake outing, you would know that it's got big, sandy beaches. But the two of you obviously had your own reasons for not wanting to come with us on *that* particular trip."

Neither Lily or I could think of a suitable response and Pit yelled at us to get moving so we did that instead.

There *was* a beach. And it was beautiful. A soft curve of palest yellow sand fringed by tall pines, which gently dropped their needles and cones on to the shady ground below. We laid out our towels. The lake was huge, like the calmest sea, turquoise in the shallow, and then suddenly, further out, the deepest, darkest blue where the bottom shelved dramatically.

Pit was right, beach volleyball was fun; everyone joined in. I wasn't too bad at it either, but Lily was sensational. She was a natural athlete. Even the cool French girls were impressed. After we had run ourselves into exhaustion on the hot sand, punching the ball with our clenched fists across the net, we collapsed in the warm, blue water.

The German boys started races with the French and English boys. The lake was very shallow for a long distance, like a giant baby pool before the "drop". I couldn't tell from Lily's face if she was relieved about this. I felt she must be, but I didn't want to even give her a look that might alert the others that anything was up.

After a while, the boys gave up on their races and joined the rest of us, lazing around in the shallows. Pit was talking to the owner of the little cabin that sold ice creams and cold drinks under the trees. The sun was burning down and I was pondering my stomach and wishing it was browner and flatter, when Tom lay on his back and sighed, "This is the life, I'm going to work on my tan so I'm irresistible at the disco." Jed followed suit, and the

pair of them drifted around the rest of us like a couple of large, floating islands.

"So who exactly goes to this disco?" Diane asked, sliding forwards on her front like a crocodile.

"Everyone," said Vicky firmly. "Well, everyone of our age, all nationalities. I asked Pit."

"You going?"

"*Of course!* You honestly think I'd stay here for two weeks only to miss the highlight! Especially now it's seriously worth my while."

Lily's eyes narrowed. "Really? Why's that, then?"

Vicky gave a secretive smile. "I've got my reasons."

"Anything to do with that French boy you were all over at the pool?" Diane asked, winking at Lily.

Vicky sat bolt upright, splashing Selina. "I was *not* all over him. He was all over *me*; wasn't he, Selina?"

Selina nodded loyally.

"I can't help it if I've made a bit more of an effort to meet people around here and am going to the disco with a gorgeous French boy."

What? My thoughts raced. *He's asked her already?* I felt a wave of disappointment.

"So he's actually invited you to go with him then, has he?" Lily edged nearer.

Vicky made a "Mmm…" sound.

"That's a yes, is it? He's asked you to go with him? *Officially?*" Lily would be a great lawyer if the acting career didn't work out.

Vicky pulled a face and sighed. "Well no, not *exactly*. Who are you, anyway? Sherlock Holmes? Not *officially*. But it's obvious he's going to. Anyway, what's it to you?"

"Nothing, nothing at all." Lily closed her eyes as if going off in a dream, before suddenly opening them again and asking airily, "So, is he staying at the campsite?"

"What! Why do you want to know so much about him?"

Lily raised her eyebrows. "Just making conversation, that's all. Showing an interest."

"Yeah, well, there's no need. But seeing as you're such a nosey parker and need to know every detail of his life – I can tell you that he's

called Jean Paul, he lives next to the stables and he's the son of the people that own them. Oh, and his friend is the campsite owner's son. Satisfied now?"

Lily blew out slowly, "Pfff, whatever," and drifted slowly back to me. She gave me a huge wink. Pit appeared at the water's edge and called us in. It was time for lunch.

Lily and I waded back together. She gleefully rubbed her hands. "Heh, heh, heh," she chortled. "Now my cunning plan begins to fall into place. We know where to find him now, don't we? *And* he's going to the disco. And, whatever Vicky says, he hasn't asked anyone yet. So anything could happen, couldn't it?"

And I had to agree that it could.

10

"If *I* can do it, Amy, *you* can."

"I can't do it."

"You can try."

"But I don't *want* to try."

Lily sighed and began again, "Was I frightened when you made me let go of the float yesterday? Was I?"

And I had to admit she was. Petrified. It was just as well the others had had enough of swimming after their day at the lake and weren't around. I'd tried to tell her that she was safe and I wouldn't let

her go, but it was like hanging on to a panic-stricken flamingo.

"But I gave it a *try*, didn't I? And no, it wasn't a one hundred per cent successful first lesson, but I'm still not giving up just because it flipped me out a bit."

I didn't answer. I'd thought she'd be easy to teach, having seen how athletic she was playing beach volleyball. I was wrong.

"And you of all people know what that's like, don't you?"

I still said nothing.

"So, like I said, if I can say I'm not giving up learning to swim, then you've got to let me help you. I love horses ... I may never have actually *been* on one, but they hold no fears for me. It'll be fine. I promise. Come to the stables with us today. Please? I'll look after you, and of course you won't have to do anything that you don't want to do. Pit will make sure you're OK, too. Come on, pleeeeease?" She began to windmill her arms in a swimming stroke imitation, before making choking, drowning noises.

"I cannot believe you're making me do this, Lily! It's practically blackmail. I'll go, but I'm only going to walk into the yard to prove I can, OK? Then I'm going; that's all."

"OK. There's another reason for you to go back, of course." She raised her eyebrows at me.

I blushed. She didn't have to tell me what that was.

I didn't tell Mum or Dad where I was going. But that afternoon, after a morning's cycling in the woods around the campsite, I found myself once more walking through the archway into the stable yard. Madame Blanc, the dark-haired woman from the other day, who I now realized was Jean Paul's mother, immediately came up and made me feel welcome.

"It's good that you came back," she said, smiling at me, and before I could back off she had taken me by the arm and, chatting away, led me towards the dusty shade of the tack room. *Great*, I thought, *she's being sensitive and taking me somewhere I'll feel safe. I'll wait here till the ride goes off and then go back to the campsite.* I was so deep in thought

that I didn't notice at first that there was someone else at the far end of the tack room, pulling riding hats down from their pegs.

It was Jean Paul. As if someone had flicked a switch, a rush of excitement flooded through me. I couldn't move. Lily calls it having a "love-shock". And when Jean Paul turned around, maybe I was imagining it, but he looked like he'd had a love-shock, too. But that had to be my romantic imagination running away with me. I breathed deeply and managed a small smile.

"This is my son, Jean Paul. He will help you find the hat that is the correct size for you." Madame Blanc smiled, looking at the two of us, and disappeared back into the yard.

"I must get the others their hats, also."

Jean Paul looked at the hat in his hands, then at me again. He stretched out a long, tanned arm and took another one off the rack. He gestured for me to come forwards until I stood right in front of him. He smiled, and holding the hat with both hands he raised it and gently placed it on my head. My hands flew up. "Oh, no, no," I muttered as he began

to adjust the straps along my cheek. "I'm not…"

"I see you before, in the car and in the pool, with your brother." He brushed his hair out of his eyes with his arm. "You not ride before? It's OK. Nothing to be afraid of. I will look after—"

"Will you hurry up in there!" Vicky was standing at the door with folded arms, tapping her foot. "There's quite a few of us you know, Amy, it's not just you. And anyway, what are you doing in here? You're not going to be riding, are you? Not after your last visit?"

The other riders began to wander into the tack room.

Vicky came and stood right up close to Jean Paul. "Me next."

He pushed a stray curl from my forehead back under my hat, then turned to find a hat for the foot-tapping Vicky. I waited by the door for Lily. After she got her hat, she came up and gave me a dig in the ribs and rolled her eyes, grinning from ear to ear.

As we wandered out she sang quietly, "He *loves* you, he *loves* you, he's gonna be your *boy*friend."

I gave her a jab with my elbow, but couldn't help grinning, until I realized I was now standing in the yard in a riding hat, and around me people were bringing horses and ponies out of the stalls. Pit came up immediately to check that I was OK. But if my heart had been beating fast enough before, it was going off the scale now. I pulled the hat off my head. "Are you all right, Amy?" she asked.

"You don't have to ride," Lily smiled, as Madame Blanc appeared with a fat little chestnut pony and indicated that Lily was to get on. "There's nothing to worry about. Just watch me. See how it's done."

I placed myself against the far wall, as out of the way as I could possibly manage.

Lily's pony was so small her long legs trailed nearly to the ground. She hadn't picked up the reins yet and, free to roam, the pony came strolling over to my wall to munch a bale of straw.

"I can't do these footrest things," Lily moaned, making frantic lunges with her feet.

I couldn't help laughing. "Stirrups," I said. "Look, you just put your foot in it. Not your whole foot to the ankle! No! Not like that! Like this!" And before

I knew what I was doing, I had put my riding hat down, reached out and guided her foot into the right position. But now I could see the stirrups were too short, her knees were up by her chin, like a jockey, so I quickly adjusted them for her. I stepped back to the safety of my wall and looked up at her. Her expression surprised me. "Relax, Lily."

"Relax! That's great coming from you!"

I blushed. "Sorry."

"No, *I'm* sorry, I shouldn't have said that. It was stupid. It's just that I've never been on a horse before … ooh, here we go again." Her pony began to move off. "Where's the stop button?"

"You told me you *loved* horses," I called after her.

"I do, but not necessarily from this angle."

A French voice cut into our conversation. "You must have ridden before." I turned to find Jean Paul watching me. "You know how to help your friend."

He stroked the neck of the dusty black pony he was leading by the reins. "Do you want…?"

I was aware that everyone else was up on their horses. A man, who I realized must be Jean Paul's father, and a stable girl were tying lead reins on to

the horses of those who hadn't ridden before.

"I know you are a bit frightened of the horse so I ask if you…" He was distracted by the sight of Lily, whose pony was ambling out of the yard with Lily helplessly flapping its reins.

"Byeee y'all!" The stable girl hurried after her and caught the bridle, turning her round. "Hellooo again," she cried. "Thank goodness we're only going for a trundle around the woods."

"Some of us will be cantering," sniffed Vicky.

Jean Paul was looking into my eyes enquiringly. There was nothing more that I wanted to do than please him, please Lily – and say yes. The heat of the stable yard suddenly seemed overwhelming and the sunlight too dazzling. The waiting horses began to stamp; a few tossed their heads.

I heard Vicky sigh. "Honestly. Are we ever going to start this ride?"

Jean Paul took a step towards me, the pony followed, and I wanted to say, "Please don't make me do this. Please. I'm frightened and I'm not ready and I don't want to say no in front of everyone and make a fool of myself all over again.

Please, *please* don't try to persuade me to get on that pony... I said I can't do it and I was right. I just can't..." But my mouth was too dry and nothing came out.

"I must go with the ride now." He smiled gently. "But if you like, while you wait for us, Nano," he patted the pony's shoulder, disturbing a cloud of dust, "has come back from her ride very, very dirty. The girl who rode her last, just leave her like this. Could you brush her? She likes it. My mother will be here with you – if you need anything." He pushed the hair out of his eyes again.

It must have been a combination of relief and the sight of him doing that, but my knees felt like they were going to give way right there.

I found my voice, "What? You don't want me to ride her? You want me to *groom* her?"

"My mother will help you."

"Oh, I don't know..."

"For God's sake, are we ever going!" Vicky snapped. Jean Paul raised his eyebrows at me, tied up Nano and leaped up on to his horse. The ride clattered off out into the summer haze.

"Byeee, Amy. Wish me luck," Lily called behind her, leaving me and Nano alone in the yard with Madame Blanc.

She handed me a brush and curry comb. "We begin, yes?"

And somehow, with just us in the yard, in the sleepy sunshine, and Nano calmly munching hay, it didn't seem quite such a terrifying thing. Madame Blanc began to make firm brushstrokes on Nano's neck; she indicated for me to follow. Tentatively I reached out and made a quick, soft brushstroke along Nano's neck. She stayed very still. I gave her another brush, then another and as I went on they got stronger and firmer, so that even when she shook her head from time to time to get rid of a fly, I stopped starting back.

It seemed so strange to be doing something so familiar, something that I had done hundreds of times before, in surroundings that I knew so well and yet were so different at the same time. After a while, I began to find the rhythm of grooming her almost soothing – to the extent that when Madame Blanc went off to answer the phone,

I was fine with it. I was almost glad it was just the two of us. Nano and me.

"You are a good girl," I crooned as I worked. "You're going to be very pretty when we're finished. You're not scary like that big grey, are you? No. You're lovely and you're going to be the shiniest pony in the stables…" Nano shook her head as if in agreement.

I don't know what else I found to talk to her about, but I do know that the sound of the ride coming back through the arch woke me as if I'd been in a dream. And I didn't know how long Madame Blanc had been standing watching me by the office door, smiling.

The noise and clamour sent me scuttling over to the sanctuary of the tack room with the excuse of putting away the grooming things.

"Nano, she looks beautiful." Jean Paul was standing at the doorway, holding his saddle and bridle. I blushed. The others started piling up behind him. I felt he wanted to say something more, but instead he wiped the damp hair off his forehead.

"You are going to the pool later?"

"Yes, we all are," Vicky said loudly, as she brushed past me. Jean Paul's grey eyes didn't move from my face.

"Yes, but, erm … I have to be in the baby pool to look after my brother."

"I come and say hello?"

"What! Wow! Yes, sure. If you like."

"I like."

I was walking on air as I left the tack room. I couldn't wait to tell Lily.

"Good day, Amy?" asked Pit, as we cycled back.

I gave myself an inner hug. "The very, very best day, thanks."

Lily and I were with Jack in the baby pool. Waiting. Lily hadn't been that keen; she said she'd feel like a gooseberry when *he* turned up. But I pleaded that I needed her moral support, and she had relented.

I hadn't told Mum or Dad about grooming Nano. To be honest, I was still going over it in my head. Anyway, I might decide never to go back to the stables again. But whatever happened, I needed it to be my decision.

I thought of how Jean Paul had pushed that stray curl back under my hat. My stomach was in knots,

as I tried not to stare at everyone coming in through the entrance to the pool.

"I don't want to look like I'm waiting for him."

"Well, swap with me. I'll let you know when he comes." Lily moved around. "See, I've got a great view now. I'll let you know as soon as I spot him."

"How?"

"How? Like this." She slapped her hands over her cheeks and began screaming hysterically, "HE'S HERE, AMY! HE'S HERE! HE'S COMING OVER, OH YES, HERE HE COMES. HE'S NEARLY HERE. ACT CASUAL!"

I gave a horrified shriek, but couldn't stop laughing.

"Trust me, I will be subtle. I must keep watch now, don't distract me." She shaded her eyes and gazed fixedly at the entrance gate.

Jack climbed up on to my shoulders. "I'm a giant, look at me, Lily!"

Lily splashed him and he began to splash her back. Water and hair were getting into my face, not to mention that I was caught in Jack's vice-like grip. I sank below the water to try and gently push

him off. Lily began to join in the game by tugging frantically at my foot, but Jack was clinging on like a limpet. I re-emerged with him still tightly clamped to my head.

"You can stop tugging now…" I spluttered.

And then I saw Lily's face. She was looking at me with a staring and desperate smile that could only mean one thing. I turned round slowly. Jack, welded to my head, turned with me and then we were both staring – straight at Jean Paul.

I removed Jack's hand from my mouth. "Hi."

"Hello," he said, and sat down on the edge of the pool.

"Jean Paul! We're over here!" It was Vicky and Selina calling from the big pool. I could see them out of the eye that Jack hadn't got his hand clamped over. Jean Paul waved cheerfully at them, but didn't move. Instead, he put his bag down and got out a Frisbee. "Your brother, he wants to play?"

"Hooray!" cried Jack, scrambling off me. "Let's play." And we did. Lily, Jack, Jean Paul and me. Then Greg turned up with the German boys and joined in, followed by Diane, Tom and Jed. Finally,

reluctantly, Vicky and Selina abandoned hopes of anyone joining them in the big pool and came over, too.

Vicky must have accidently on purpose "bumped" into Jean Paul a hundred times trying to snatch the Frisbee from him. In her expensive pink bikini, she looked amazing. She was relaxed and laughing and making jokes about how bad she was at the game and how the boys weren't being fair on her. Jean Paul, however, seemed more concerned that Jack wasn't left out, and made sure he threw to him whenever he could. And to me.

When we all sat down for a drink on the grass, Tom said, "Why don't we all meet up in the square in front of the café tonight? We could have a rematch!"

"Sure thing," replied Jed.

"You're joking," Diane laughed. "More of this torture? But it would be cool to meet up. We could have a drink in the café."

Vicky looked straight at Jean Paul and gave him a flirty smile. "Can you come?"

He paused for a moment, before nodding his head. "Sure, I will come."

"At last, Amy!" Lily was hopping about next to me on the way back to our tents. "Time to just chill out with Jean Paul."

"But what about Vicky? I can't see her letting that happen."

"I'll just have to distract her. We'll think of something to keep her busy. Don't worry about that now. The important thing is that you're going to spend an evening with him. Will your parents be OK with you going out?"

"Sure, it'll be fine," I said happily.

But I was wrong.

"Amy, you promised you'd look after Jack tonight!" said Mum. "You know you did. We asked you two days ago and you said it would be no problem. And we've bought the tickets now."

It was true, but in all the excitement I'd completely forgotten. "But Mum! I've *got* to go and meet the others tonight. I've just got to! It was you who said you wanted me to make friends here. I have to go. Can't you go to this opera thing another night?"

"You heard Mum, we've bought the tickets. We have to go tonight. There'll be other nights for you to meet your friends, Amy," Dad said soothingly.

"No there won't!" I wailed. But how could I explain to him that if I didn't meet up with the others tonight, it would be too late. I had seen Vicky flirting with Jean Paul all afternoon. And now she would have a whole evening with him. And I could do nothing about it.

Why was life so unfair?

12

"Amy? Are you in there?"

It was Lily. I opened the tent flap and put my finger to my lips. "Shh, Jack's just gone to sleep."

"Are you coming?"

"I *can't*. I've got to stay here and babysit."

"What?!" she hissed. "But what about Jean Paul? He'll think you're not interested."

"Yes, thank you for reminding me," I whispered bitterly. "I totally forgot I'd promised Mum. Will you try and let him know – *in a non-obvious way*," I gave her a special look, "why I'm not there?"

"Of course," said Lily. Then another thought struck her. "Wow. Vicky's going to be all over him…"

"*I know!*" I said miserably. "I think this evening was my last chance. I might as well accept the fact he's not going to be able to resist her. She's so confident and pretty."

"We've talked about this already!" Lily responded assertively. "So are you! You've got beautiful hair and amazing blue eyes. You're sporty and funny. He'd be mad not to like you best. Look, if you're not going, I'm not going. I'll stay here and we can babysit Jack together. Let's sit outside where we can stop whispering and talk instead." She plonked herself down on one of the folding chairs and said, "Now tell me why on earth you think that Vicky stands a better chance than you?"

"Duh – Lily, are you serious? Look at her. And I've got hardly any experience of boys and she's obviously got loads. I don't know how to flirt and I wouldn't know what to do if a boy I liked actually liked *me*. I bet she's kissed a hundred boys."

"Have you?"

"What?"

"Ever kissed a boy?"

I went pink. "Yes, of course I have. Have you?"

"Of course!"

"What was it like?"

Lily took a deep breath. "It was absolutely the most wonderful, dreamy experience of my life." She was watching my reaction out of the corner of her eye. "The most heart-stopping, romantic thing that has ever happened to me. I shall never, ever forget it."

"Wow," I whistled softly. "I shall never, ever forget mine, either. It was fantastic."

There was a moment's silence. We listened to the crickets singing in the warm evening air.

Lily broke first. "Yours was rubbish, wasn't it? I hope so. Because mine was."

"It was awful!" I groaned. "It wasn't even a kiss. I ducked and he slurped my forehead."

Lily shrieked with laughter. "Mine is so, so much worse. He was a foot shorter than me, and we were slow dancing at a party when he unexpectedly decided to go for it. His head shot up, banged my chin and I bit my tongue. It was the

most embarrassing experience of my life. I never saw him again. I mean that's not even close to a kiss, is it? That's grievous bodily harm."

"I bet no one's ever slurped on Vicky's forehead," I sighed.

"Hey, you're lucky you even had a slurp. I *dream* of a slurp. A slurp would be, like, a *huge* advance for us tongue-biters."

"Well, you'll just have to kiss taller boys, Lily." I tapped my finger on my cheek and tipped my head to one side. "Mmm … taller boys. Now I wonder where we could find one of those…"

Lily looked puzzled. "What are you talking about?"

"A certain very tall boy, who, now that he's not so shy, is actually really nice and rather dishy. Who looks at you like *this*." I lolled my head forward and made goo-goo eyes in her face.

She reared back in her chair, blushing. "I don't know *who* you're talking about."

"Come on! You must have seen Greg's expression when he looks at you – he absolutely fancies you."

"No, he doesn't. What are you talking about! You've gone completely mad!" Lily shrieked, jumped up and ran around the table a couple of times, giggling and madly waving her hands, before collapsing back into her chair. She rolled her head in my direction.

"Do you *really* think he likes me?"

"Yes, I do."

"But *why?*" she said, suddenly anxious. "I'm too tall and gangly and I've got orange hair…" She gave it a tug.

And I suddenly realized that I had been so wrapped up in my own problems and dramas that I hadn't given much thought to what Lily might be hoping or feeling … or what she might be missing by sitting with me outside my tent.

I got up, stood behind her chair and began to tip her out. "Time to go now, Lily. I'll not have you staying here another minute. I've got a great book I want to read, and you have some major boy-action waiting for you."

"But I don't know what to *doooo*. I'm good at telling other people, but I can't do it myself."

"My friend Sasha says there are three kissing rules."

She leaned forward eagerly. "Tell me, tell me."

I took a deep breath. "They are:

1. Relax

2. Close your eyes

3. Enjoy."

Lily's lip curled. "Is that it? Tell your friend Sasha that that's the biggest pile of rubbish advice I've ever heard."

"It's all you need."

"No it's not. It's no help at all, is it? What about nose position, breathing and teeth clashing? All possible areas of potential disaster."

"Sasha says that if you stop thinking about it, it'll just work out."

"Well, good for her. But some of us might need a bit more direction than that. What do *you* think?"

"*I* don't know – I'm Miss 'Drool on Forehead', remember? But you'll never find out if you don't get moving! Get going!"

"I feel bad leaving you."

"Don't. Go! Now!"

I gave her a push and she set off. She turned round and started walking backwards.

"I'll try to tell Jean Paul for you."

"Thanks."

She turned and disappeared into the evening, and I went to lie on my camp bed, dreaming of Sasha's rules in a Jean Paul situation. I hoped with all my heart that, somewhere on the other side of the campsite, my fragile hopes were not being destroyed as I lay there.

I was up early, nervously pacing around outside the tent, willing Lily to appear. I had to find out what had happened last night.

At last she came into view, and as she walked towards me, I could tell from just looking at her that the news wasn't great.

"Was she all over him?" I asked, as I got up to walk our now familiar route to the clubhouse.

Lily screwed up her nose. "She was a bit."

"How bad was it? Did you get to speak to him? Did you tell him why I wasn't there?"

"I tried, but it was difficult to get near him with Velcro Girl stuck to his side all evening … and you did say don't make it *obvious*. I did try to throw it into the conversation, but as they weren't really talking to anyone else, I'm not sure if it was fully understood. Uh oh, coming up on the left-hand side, smug friends alert…"

"Hiya, girls," Vicky sang breezily, as she and Selina caught up with us.

"Hiya," we chorused listlessly.

"Isn't it just the most gorgeous day?"

"Isn't it though?" Lily replied. "Do you know what it reminds me of? Yesterday. No, I mean the day before that. In fact, goodness, every day we've had since we've been here."

Vicky slapped her arm. "You are so funny!"

Even Lily was surprised by this uncharacteristic cheer.

"What are we doing today?" Selina asked.

"Tennis," Vicky answered immediately. "All morning – and the afternoon off today. Which is just as well." She gave a smug smile and twirled her hair around her fingers.

No one asked why. Selina obviously already knew, and from the expression on Lily's face I didn't want to know. I wanted to put my hands over my ears.

"Got to get changed after tennis. I'm meeting up with Jean Paul later. He's out on rides all morning. But then we're spending the afternoon together."

We were at the clubhouse door.

I stopped dead. "You go in," I said to Lily. "I'm not feeling so good."

"Amy, come on…"

"No, Lily, seriously, I don't feel great." I managed to force a smile. "You go and have a great time, I'll see you later. I still need to hear all about *your* evening, Lily…"

But she gave me a massive warning look and I closed my mouth. "See you later, then."

They disappeared into the clubhouse.

I felt such a fool. What had I been thinking, imagining he liked me. Even if he had, he had hardly felt very strongly about me. Vicky had spent one evening with him and he'd forgotten that I existed. I felt stupidly like crying, which was why I

hadn't gone into the clubhouse. I knew I was being a bit of a wimp, but I couldn't spend a morning listening to her talking about it.

I didn't know what to do next, so I wandered back to the tent. I knew it was ridiculous to feel so disappointed about a boy I hardly knew. Had I been so wrong, thinking there was a connection between us yesterday? Had I made it too obvious I liked him? I didn't think so. Or had he just decided that, having spent time with me, he wasn't that interested? Miserable and confused, I arrived back at the tent to find it was deserted.

Mum and Dad had taken Jack to his club, so I picked up my bike and set off, with no idea of where I was going. I knew I should have left a note for them, but then they'd think something was up and I didn't want to have to offer any explanations.

I cycled out of the campsite, past the stables and into the countryside. I kept going into the next village, past the supermarket, and I had reached the borders of the little town when I realized it was a long distance to cycle back, so I turned round. I wondered what Lily would say to me. Probably

that I was making a big deal out of something very small and that I needed to pull myself together and get things in perspective. I pulled my shoulders back and began to cycle more calmly. She was right. I wasn't going to be stupid about it. It wasn't that important.

I don't know what made me turn into the stables as I came down the last road. I placed my bike against the stone wall and walked through the arch. The yard was silent and empty. A sleepy ginger cat, basking on a bench, acknowledged my arrival with a twitch of its tail. Then Nano put her head over her stable door.

I walked slowly up to her. "Hello," I said softly. She nuzzled my cheek. "You *are* a lovely pony, aren't you?"

"Do you want to groom her again?"

I jumped. Madame Blanc was standing behind me.

I found myself blushing. I nodded.

She put down the bucket she was carrying, opened Nano's door and led her out by her halter, before tying it up on one of the large iron rings in the old wall.

I was soon into the dreamy rhythm of brushing her coat, lost in thought. At last, I stood back to check my handiwork. I gazed around the stable yard, enjoying the familiar sights and smells. The only sound was the occasional rustling of a horse moving slowly around its stall and the buzzing of the odd fly … then suddenly, a tinkling noise pierced the sleepy air. Lily flew through the arch, her thumb on the bicycle bell.

"I've been looking everywhere for you," she cried, leaning her bike up against a hay bale. "Might've guessed you'd be here."

"Why aren't you at tennis?"

"They changed it to swimming."

"How did you guess?"

"What?"

"How did you guess I'd be here?"

"Because you obviously love horses – that's why."

"Would you like to ride Nano, now that you've groomed her?" Madame Blanc had reappeared. She was slipping off Nano's halter and putting a bridle on her.

"No! No! I mean no *thank you*, Madame Blanc."

"She's very gentle. I will lead you."

"No, honestly."

"Well, I'll have a go," Lily volunteered.

Madame Blanc smiled. "You can go together. She's easily strong enough for the two of you. No problem."

"Go on, Amy," Lily urged. "Just for a minute. I'll hold on to you really tightly."

I actually laughed. "*You're* going to look after *me?*"

"Oh, hark at her, we're quite the showjumper of the year now, aren't we? Just get on, will you."

I couldn't believe it. I was actually tempted. Just to feel what it was like to be back on a horse again. Nano nuzzled my cheek as if to say, "Go on, it'll be all right."

"You get on first, then," I said, my heart pounding.

Madame Blanc fetched us both riding hats, and helped Lily up – once again doing her hysterical flamingo impression. But at least with no saddle, she didn't have the stirrups to do battle with. Eventually Lily was settled. She stared down at me. "Come on then, Amy. Get your bum up here."

Madame Blanc helped me up, holding firmly on

to the reins all the time, but she didn't have to. Nano stood quite still. My heart was still thumping, but I realized that it wasn't all fear. I was excited, too. Madame Blanc asked if she could walk us a few steps around the yard. Lily's arms flew around my waist like someone on the back of a motorbike. At first I held tightly on to Nano's long, black mane, but when Madame Blanc, still holding on to the bridle, handed me the reins, my fingers slipped into the correct position automatically. It's true what people say: once you can ride, you never forget.

"Shall we gallop, Amy? Shall we?" Lily cried enthusiastically, bouncing up and down.

"No!" I laughed, exhilarated. "You can barely stay on at *this* snail's pace."

"Trot then? Canter?"

"No. We'll fall off."

Madame Blanc had taken us out of the stable yard now, and we were walking slowly past the dungheap. The low hum of flies filled the air.

"So, what happened with Greg, then?" I asked.

"We talked." She took her hand off my waist and batted it in the air. "Go away, wasp!"

"Oh you *talked*, did you?"

"Yes, we talked. And that's all we did, but ... hang on, this wasp won't leave me alone..."

"*But?* But what?" I asked, impatient to hear more. "It's a fly, ignore it." Nano shook her head in agreement.

"It's a fly in a wasp suit, then. Can't you hear it?"

"No, stop wriggling, you'll tip over."

But Lily gave a loud shriek and lunged away from her attacker. She began to slide slowly off to one side. "Save me, Amy, I'm falling!" she giggled, clutching my waist and pulling me over inch by inch.

"Let go, Lily!"

"No, I can still save myself! I must hang on!" she wailed, laughing.

But she couldn't and very slowly we slid sideways on to the soft, straw-filled warmth of the dungheap. Madame Blanc and Nano looked at each other as if to say, "You two have to be the silliest girls we've ever met."

I staggered up and looked at Lily; she was covered with straw and dung.

She began to brush down the back of her

shorts. "Are you all right, Amy? You should be, I broke your fall."

"Not if I'm in the same state as you," I said, staring at her.

She looked over my shoulder. "Oh no! Don't look now, but this could be shaping up *not* to be the best moment of your life."

I turned round. Vicky and Jean Paul were putting their bikes up against the wall. Jean Paul said coolly, "You OK?"

"Yes, a bit mucky, but we're fine." I could hardly look at him. It hurt too much to see Vicky standing next to him. "I'm sorry I missed meeting up with everybody last night," I added quickly.

He shrugged dismissively. "You had other things you wanted to do. I hope you had a nice time." He turned away.

"What?"

He began to walk off. "I hear you don't want to come out with us because you are with a boy…"

"What!" I gasped. "Who told you that?"

Jean Paul looked at Vicky, who suddenly found the brickwork on the nearby wall fascinating.

"Oh, did I get that wrong?" she said airily, turning back to me. "Lily kept trying to say something, but I obviously didn't catch the whole story. Sorry."

Jean Paul looked round at me again.

"I *was* with a boy," I said, looking straight at him. "My brother, I had to look after him. I *wanted* to come out, but I couldn't."

Jean Paul's face was expressionless for a moment, and then it broke into a big grin. "I am very happy." He checked himself. "I, er ... it is very good that you are riding the horse again, Amy."

"Hardly," Vicky snapped, looking me up and down and wrinkling her nose. "Come on, we'll be late for my first lesson." She turned back to us and said with a giggle, "Jean Paul is going to be giving me private lessons to make sure my riding skills don't get rusty. I'm practically going to be living here; you'll be quite sick of me, won't you, Jean Paul?" But he had bent down to pick up my riding hat, so I couldn't see his expression.

"I'm sick of you already," Lily muttered, as Madame Blanc helped us get back on.

My mind was racing with so many thoughts that I didn't even notice that I had gathered up Nano's reins and ridden her back to the stable yard myself until I'd dismounted and was helping Lily off.

"Look at you!" Lily smiled. "Brilliant! But what's not so great is how we smell."

Madame Blanc took us to the sink in the tack room and handed us a bar of strong-smelling soap.

"Don't think I've forgotten your news in all that excitement, Lily. So come on. 'But' what?"

"What are you on about? 'But' what?" Lily replied.

"You said you and Greg only talked, '*but*'... 'But' what?"

She blushed happily. "*But* he did ask me if I was going to the disco. And then he said he hoped I was!"

"Aaaargh!" I shrieked. "He *loves* you, he *loves* you, he's gonna be your *boy*friend. What did I tell you?"

"Well, what about *you*?"

"I don't know what you're talking about!" I protested, laughing. "Come on, we'd better go back and get out of these clothes." As we left the stables and went to collect our bikes, Jean Paul came running out through the archway. "Amy, wait, please!"

I felt a rush of excitement, but tried to keep calm. Which was more than Lily did; she was standing behind Jean Paul and looking at me over his shoulder. "He *loves* you," she mouthed slowly, before tactfully drawing her bike to one side.

Jean Paul stood in front of me, and I don't know if it was the heat of the sun or what, but it was as if there was a warm magnetic field around him, drawing me in.

"I speak with my mother, she says I can take you riding tomorrow. If you like. You pay nothing. You ride Nano today, and it's very important that you ride again very soon. You can come?"

My heart did a wild, happy dance.

"OK. I'd like that. If you're sure?"

"Sure I am sure. I *like*."

I knew I was blushing. "What time?"

He looked back into the stable yard, where Vicky was already up on her horse. "I come to the pool tomorrow after your club, we go then."

"OK," I said. "See you tomorrow."

Lily and I climbed on to our bikes, and had to pretend to cycle casually along the road until we were out of sight. Then we whizzed around in an hysterical dance of celebration.

14

"Will it *ever* be this afternoon?" I asked Lily, as we pushed open the door to Teen Club. "I don't think I can wait."

Just then, Selina burst into the clubhouse behind us with the news that two new English boys had arrived in the tent next to hers last night. They were called Finn and Charlie, and they were friends on holiday with Finn's family. And they were gorgeous!

"And they're down to start the club today," Pit interrupted, coming up to us with her clipboard.

"This morning we're going to the adventure park, where it will be all climbing, balancing and rope work high up in the trees. Don't worry, you'll all be in safety harnesses, so if you fall you'll only dangle around a bit. Oh, hello…" Pit paused as a dark head peered around the door. "Welcome. I'm afraid introductions will have to take place on the minibus; we're running late."

"Where's Vicky?" Tom asked, looking round.

"Not feeling great today. Says she'll probably be back tomorrow," Pit said, as she shooed everyone out.

The two new boys slid into the seats opposite Lily and me on the bus. A year or two older than us, Finn had thick, dark, wavy hair, an easy smile and sleepy brown eyes. Charlie was taller, his straight, brown hair hung nearly to his shoulders. He grinned confidently at his new surroundings, then stared straight at me with sharp, blue eyes.

"So what goes on around here?" he asked.

"Well, there's the lake and cycling and the pool for starters…" I began.

"And what about evening entertainment?"

"There's the funfair tomorrow. You must've seen the posters around the campsite. It's just a local one, but everyone's going. It should be a good evening."

"I shall look forward to it, then." He grinned.

Charlie was exactly the sort of boy that Sasha usually went for – sure of himself, relaxed and handsome. Boys like that go for girls like Sasha. But this boy for some reason went for *me*. At first I thought I was imagining it, but it soon became clear that he was making a big effort to flatter and impress. I could sense Lily's amusement next to me the whole bumpy journey; she said nothing, but every so often I felt her elbow digging into my side.

When we got to the adventure park, we put our harnesses on, and started climbing up through the ropes and swinging bridges in the forest. It was terrifying at first. But not for Charlie. He soon established himself as leader of the pack, standing high up in the trees on a rope bridge, swinging it dangerously to and fro and laughing at the efforts of Tom and Jed below, as they puffed their way slowly up a rope ladder.

"Come on! What are you like? Tweedledum and Tweedledee. What have you got to be afraid of? You'd bounce if you fell. Not like you, Greg, eh?"

Greg looked up from where he was tentatively crossing a bridge of swinging poles.

"It's like watching a stick insect walk across a twig!"

Tom and Jed pretended to laugh. Greg ignored him, but you could see he was annoyed. Charlie was mistaken if he thought that I was impressed by his "funny" jokes. Quite the opposite. He was good looking, but he was also arrogant and unkind.

Everyone did much more than they thought they could. (Although Greg and Lily spent a great deal of time getting stuck in the same trees.) Even Tom and Jed finished the course eventually. It would have been better without Charlie's stupid comments, though.

As soon as the minibus pulled up back at the campsite, I ran to get changed to go to the pool.

I put on my brand-new, blue bikini I had persuaded Mum to buy me as a reward for

babysitting and headed for the baby pool. Lily and I had decided to hang out there so that we could both keep a lookout for each other. Lily had her own reason now for keeping an eye on the pool entrance.

"So come on, Lily. What was all that getting stuck in the same tree business this morning. I'd like all the details, please…"

"Hello!"

I turned round. Charlie and Finn were standing at the poolside. "Come and swim with us in the big pool."

I looked at Lily. "Er … no thanks, we're fine here." But then all the others, including Vicky, appeared. She had obviously made a full recovery.

I saw Lily's face light up when she saw Greg. "Come on, you haven't got Jack to look after, have you? What's stopping you?" Greg pleaded. But he was looking at Lily.

Lily leaned forward and hissed, "Let's go."

"What? But you can't…"

"I'll hang around the edge; I won't actually, you know … *swim*. I'll be fine. Come on."

I knew she really wanted to be with Greg and there was no sign of Jean Paul, so we clambered out and joined the others.

As soon as I got in the big pool, I wished I hadn't. Charlie just wouldn't leave me alone. First he showed off his diving, then he started bombing the other boys with massive crashing jumps. It was impossible to swim properly, so in the end I gave up and got out. He followed me in a flash, walking alongside me, grinning dangerously, as I wandered towards Greg and Lily, who were lying on their towels, chatting.

"Don't tell me you've had enough, Amy!" Charlie gasped in mock surprise.

"I just want a bit of a breather."

"I think you need cooling off!" He grabbed my arm and began to pull me towards the pool.

"No!" I cried and pulled away.

"Oh, I think *yes*!" He yelled triumphantly and grabbed me closer. Suddenly, with a strong lunge, he had scooped me off my feet and was carrying me off the grass and across the concrete stones surrounding the pool.

"Put me down!" I kicked my legs, but found myself automatically clinging to his neck. I was terrified he was going to drop me on to the hard ground. He got to the edge of the pool and jumped in with me still in his arms. Once I felt the safety of being under water, I kicked out firmly and swam with strong, angry strokes to the surface. Charlie surfaced next to me, spluttering and laughing loudly. I shook the hair off my face, and looking up noticed a figure standing at the poolside. It was Jean Paul, and he did not look amused.

15

"Is that boy your friend?" he asked as we cycled out of the campsite.

"No! Definitely not. He just arrived today. I've never met him before."

Jean Paul raised his eyebrows. "He behaves like he knows you well. He likes you, no?"

"I don't know. Like I said, I only met him this morning. I'm not sure if he's a very nice person."

Jean Paul perked up. "Non?"

"Non," I replied firmly.

I could hardly believe it, but I was actually

looking forward to getting back on Nano. Me! Who only a short while ago had yelled at Mum and Dad for even suggesting I went *near* the stables.

I wondered what they would say if they could have seen me ride Nano into the outdoor riding school. Jean Paul asked me to walk her round a few times, and with each circuit I felt my confidence grow. He walked alongside me, asking me to stop Nano every so often; she always obeyed immediately. Then he went into the middle and watched me for a while.

"You OK to trot now?" he asked.

I nodded. Nano responded at once to my gentle kick and I found myself rising and falling in the saddle like I had done hundreds of times before. Once again, Jean Paul asked me to slow down to a walk every so often, then start to trot again.

"Canter!" Jean Paul shouted, and I sank into the familiar lilting gait; now I knew that Nano would stop when I asked her, I could let myself go and enjoy the speed and rhythm of the ride as we cantered first in circles, then figures of eight.

"Whoa!" Jean Paul cried. I pulled Nano gently to

a halt next to where he was standing in the centre. I couldn't help it, I was laughing with surprise and happiness. He patted Nano's neck. He looked puzzled. "Amy, you ride very well. Why did you not want to ride before; why are you afraid?"

He must have seen the expression on my face as he took the reins and gestured for me to dismount. "We have a break now. You are tired. You are hungry? I have bread."

I slid off and he tied Nano up by the water trough. He was right, I did suddenly feel tired, and hungry. He went to fetch his backpack, which was hanging on the gate, and threw it on to the ground. He sank down, leaned against the fence and made himself comfortable. He patted the ground next to him and I sat down, so close my shoulder was nearly touching his. He got out a bottle of water, a baguette and some slices of ham and made a giant sandwich.

He saw me smile. "You think I am not a very good chef, hey?" he said, breaking it in two and offering me half.

I grinned and took a bite. "It's the best sandwich

I've ever had," I sighed. And I wasn't lying.

He leaned back, enjoying the sun on his face as we ate in companionable silence. When we had finished, he said, "So, you tell me now. About what happened to you that made you afraid to ride?"

"It's a long story."

"I want to hear everything. From the beginning."

So I took a deep breath and I told him. I told him everything, just as I'd told Lily. About the misty morning, about the noise of the cars, about pulling the horses into the verge, the horror of the crash, the crack on my skull and waking up in hospital and the long, lonely weeks recovering afterwards.

When I had finished he was silent for a while, then he leaned towards me, so his shoulder was touching mine. His grey eyes were serious. He lifted up my hair and looked at the thin scar, before gently letting it go.

"And your horse?"

I froze. "What?" I pretended I hadn't heard properly. I needed time to think.

Nobody had ever asked about her before. I've had to tell a lot of people about the accident, but

they never, ever think to ask what happened to Mitzi. And I never tell them. The people that know what happened to her that morning were told not to talk about it. It was a taboo subject around me. But here was Jean Paul asking me the question I most dreaded. He said it again.

"What happened to your horse? Was she OK?"

And maybe it was because I was tired, maybe it was because of riding Nano, I'm not sure, but for the first time I allowed myself to think about Mitzi and not immediately fight to drive those memories away. Instead, I let her flow into my head: how she was my favourite, how brave she was and how good. How she used to nuzzle my coat for treats, the way she shook her head when she was happy, like she had done that morning, just before … just before she was gone. And I knew that I had truly, truly loved her. And suddenly I knew I missed her more than I could possibly say. I felt tears beginning to well up in my eyes.

Jean Paul sat up. "Amy," he touched my arm, "Amy, I'm sorry, I didn't mean to make you sad. What is the matter?"

But the tears were pouring down my cheeks now, and I could feel the big choking sobs that were to come.

"Is it my question? About the horse?" His face was full of concern. "Something happen?"

I nodded dumbly, then caught the first waves of shaking tears with my hands over my face. He reached out and put his arm around me.

"Tell me."

I lifted up my head and fought to get the words out through my tears.

"She was hurt?"

At last I choked them out.

"She died!" It felt like I was wailing it out to the trees and the sky and the whole wide world.

"She died," I cried again. And Jean Paul's arm went tight around me and I cried into his shoulder like I would never stop.

But eventually there were no tears left. I pulled away, embarrassed.

"I'm sorry," I sniffed, searching around for something to wipe my face on. "That wasn't meant to happen. That was awful. Sorry."

He rummaged in his bag and handed me a T-shirt. He saw my expression. "Go on, it's dirty anyway." He smiled. Then he offered me a drink of water. It tasted cold and sweet.

"Tell me about Mitzi. What was she like?"

To my surprise, I found I could talk about her.

"She was good, very lively but always did what you asked of her."

"So a good pony. No naughty tricks?" he asked.

I found myself laughing. "She had some tricks she used to play on me, like pickpocketing the carrots from my jeans when I was grooming her."

"Did you ride her every time, or other horses, too?"

"Other horses, too, but she was my favourite in the stables."

"Tell me about these stables. Were they like this one?"

So I talked about my old life and how I thought I could never go back. As I told Jean Paul all about it, I realized how much I missed it.

"Do you think you go back to your old stables now?" he asked.

I took a deep breath and managed a smile. "Maybe, you know. Maybe."

"And now you must ride some more. We are not finished. Allez!"

He stood up and, taking my hand, pulled me to my feet. And it was the strangest thing, but I felt as light as a feather, as if a huge load had been taken off me. I practically floated back on to Nano.

Jean Paul made Nano and me work hard for another half-hour of walking, trotting and cantering, first one way, then the next, stopping and starting, stirrups crossed, arms folded. He put us both through our paces and I could feel my old confidence coming back, stronger and stronger. Eventually he signalled it was time to finish. As I dismounted and landed next to him, I said shyly, "Thanks."

"Why you thank me? I make you work hard." He smiled, lifting Nano's reins over her head.

I blushed. "You know, for everything."

He looked at me, reaching out to briefly touch my forehead. "You know, Amy, you think you are afraid, but really you are a very, very brave girl..."

I shook my head.

"But tomorrow we will see how really brave you are."

I looked puzzled.

"At the fair?" He grinned. "You will come?"

"Yes… I—"

I was interrupted by a loud rattling noise. Vicky was announcing her arrival by banging her riding crop against the fence. But this time her presence didn't make me feel anxious or threatened. We walked towards her. Her irritated expression turned into a beaming smile as Jean Paul got close.

"Hi, Jean Paul! Here for my lesson, right on time. What were you two talking about that was so interesting?"

"We were talking about the funfair," I answered.

Vicky looked at Jean Paul. "Are you going?"

Jean Paul looked at me and grinned. "Yes," we said together.

Vicky raised her eyebrows at me. "Well we all know *you're* going, Amy. It's all around the campsite. Charlie's told everyone."

"Told everyone what?"

Amy

"That you said you'd go with him."

"I didn't!" I gasped. "I never said that!"

Vicky's hands flew up in front of her. "OK, OK, if you don't want to admit it. But I can't see the point in denying it. Charlie's told everyone you said you'd go with him."

"That's just nonsense," I spluttered. Vicky rolled her eyes at Jean Paul. "Oh dear, I seem to have spoken out of turn. Sorry, Amy, I didn't mean to blab your business all over the place. Anyway…" she continued, slapping her crop against the fence again, "…I'd love to stand and chat, but isn't it time for my lesson? And I think I might actually be *paying* for mine?"

Jean Paul handed me Nano's reins, expressionless, and walked off with Vicky towards the stables. I stood there rooted to the spot, watching them go. How dare she! But just as I was about to boil over with frustration, he turned around, caught my eye and gave me a huge wink.

I winked back and gave Nano the biggest hug she'd ever had.

16

"Don't you worry about what they get up to?"

"What?!" I yelled. The music from the dodgems was competing with the cheesy tunes from every other ride and I could hardly hear Charlie, even though he was shouting.

"Vicky and Jean Paul, during those 'private'…" Charlie made inverted comma signs with his fingers, "…riding lessons. Aren't you worried he's having fun playing you both off against each other?"

I was still furious with Charlie for telling everyone

that we were going to the fair together. I had just arrived with Mum and Jack, who had disappeared into the crowds towards the merry-go-round. We'd all agreed to meet at the dodgems, and Charlie had been the first one there, leaning against a caravan. I didn't want to talk to him, so I was relieved to see the others pushing their way through the crowds towards us.

"Hello, Amy!" the German boys chorused. "We are challenging the twins to battle on the dodgems. Be warned. It shall be dangerous."

"Who're you going on with?" Vicky asked.

"Erm ... not sure." I searched the crowd and my heart skipped to see Jean Paul waving as he approached. The dodgem ride ended and the cars came to a halt like balloons that had run out of air.

I jumped into an empty one and Jean Paul got in next to me. Vicky glared at us and clambered angrily into a car with Selina. One of the Dutch girls jumped in next to Charlie, and as the ride began I forgot about everything but having fun. Tom and Jed managed to squish into one car and were lethal against the German boys. Diane and

Finn, Lily and Greg, and eventually even Vicky and Selina also joined in the mad battle. I couldn't remember when I had felt so happy.

It was only a scruffy local French funfair, lit up with drunken strings of fairy lights and brash electric signs for the rides, with their badly-drawn cowboys, ghosts and girls. But it was brilliant! The sticky sweet smell of candyfloss, nuts slowly roasted in caramel, hot dogs and popcorn assaulted our noses in waves. There were wild waltzers with crazy French fairground boys leaping from car to car, a helter-skelter and a large, creaking Ferris wheel. We moved in a pack from ride to ride.

Jean Paul and I went on every ride together, crushing up against each other as the waltzer span us around, before heading back to the dodgems for a rematch. The others began to peel off and go on different rides, but Vicky doggedly stuck with us, dragging the long-suffering Selina with her. When we got back to the dodgems, she jumped in one and called out for Jean Paul to join her. He appeared not to hear her over the loud fairground

music, and she sat fuming with her arms crossed for the whole ride while Selina drove.

When we staggered off, Jean Paul had to reach out a helping hand to extract Tom and Jed, who had got wedged in and were waving their arms around pleading for help. As we came down the wooden steps, I saw Jack standing there, watching. I looked around for Mum. She had promised not to be embarrassing and she had been very good at not coming up to talk to me when I was with the others. She was puffing towards us now, calling, "Jack! You *must* wait for me!"

Jean Paul leaned down to talk to him. "Do you want to go on the dodgems?"

Jack chewed his collar. "Well," he said solemnly, wincing as two cars shuddered into the barrier near us, "I would like to. But Spider Monkey doesn't want to."

And he blew out his cheeks and shrugged his shoulders in a "so what can you do?" manner.

"Amy, Amy!" Mum had reached us. "I'm *so* glad to find you. Isn't this hell on earth?" My mum is not a great lover of funfairs. "My head is going

to explode. Would you mind looking after Jack, just for twenty minutes? I'll send Dad straight here as soon as I get back to the tent. Please? This is killing me and Jack is desperate to stay a little bit longer. If your friend doesn't mind?" she added, which was practically blackmail as she was basically threatening that if I didn't say yes, she was going to strike up a conversation with Jean Paul and try and persuade him instead. He smiled at Jack.

"OK, Mum, but please, make sure Dad comes immediately; you know he moves at a snail's pace."

"Cross my heart. Amy, you're an angel." And she disappeared into the crowd.

"Do you want to come with us to the ghost train, Jean Paul?" Vicky asked. "Amy's brother's a little young for it. We could meet up with her later."

"No, I'm OK," he replied.

Charlie and the twins wandered over. "We'll go, come on." Vicky pulled a face, but she had no choice but to turn on her heel and head off with them.

Jack was thrilled to be with Jean Paul. We took

him on the little aeroplane ride and the train ride and waved dutifully every time he came around. Then he wanted an ice cream. Not popcorn, not candyfloss. Ice cream. And of course the queue for that was a mile long, but luckily next to it was a man juggling flaming clubs, who was brilliant. We must have watched mesmerized for a couple of minutes, before the queue shuffled forwards. I looked down. Jack was gone.

I didn't panic at first; I was more exasperated that we had to relinquish our place in the line as we began to search the immediate area. No one in the queue had seen a small, blond boy. Like us, they had been watching the fire juggler. After the first few minutes of searching and shouting, a nagging fear began to invade me. We came across Vicky, Selina, Greg, Lily and the twins eating hot dogs, sitting on the steps by the carousel.

"We've got to split up and search; we'll cover more ground that way than if we search together," said Greg. "Meet back here in ten minutes and tell any of the others that you see to look for him, too. Don't worry, Amy, I'm sure he's fine."

But it was now more than ten minutes since he had disappeared and Jack was in a strange environment and completely on his own. Wherever he was, I knew this much about my brother, he would *not* be "fine".

"Amy," Jean Paul said. "I have an idea to help find Jack. I will be back soon; you keep looking here, OK?"

I nodded and started to run frantically all over the fairground, but Jack was nowhere, and no one appeared to have seen a young boy wandering on his own. Suddenly the bright lights and loud music didn't seem warm and friendly any more, but confusing and menacing.

I stopped to catch my breath in front of the dodgems. Diane and Finn joined me, shaking their heads. Where had Jean Paul gone? He had said that he'd be back soon. Jack had been gone too long. Much too long. I knew there was only one thing to do now. We were going to have to call the police. But I needed someone who spoke French to call them. I needed Jean Paul. Dad was going to be here any minute. What was *he* going to say?

I felt sick. It was all my fault; I hadn't looked after Jack. Where could he be?

"Amy! Amy!" I heard a voice calling me over the relentless, cheerful din around me.

"Amy!"

I looked around wildly, but I couldn't see who was calling.

"We're over here!" I recognized a girl's voice.

"We've found him!" It was Lily and Greg. Lily was carrying a tearful Jack in her arms.

"Jack, Jack!" I cried, as he transferred himself, sniffing, from her arms into mine. "Where *were* you? Everyone's been looking *everywhere*."

"He was under the helter-skelter," Greg said.

"Jack, what on earth were you doing there? Why did you go off?"

The rest of the group was arriving now, their faces breaking into smiles on seeing Jack safe.

Jack sniffed again. "I saw a boy with a Scooby Doo toy, I mean a big one, an' I just thought I'll go an' ask him where he won it, so I could win one. So I followed him, but I couldn't keep up and then I didn't know where I was, so I did what Mum said."

"And what was that?"

"She said it to Dad when we went to the maze. If you get lost, get to a high place."

"Yes, but on *top* of a high place, not *under* it. And that's not what five-year-olds should do."

"I couldn't find a policeman or a teacher," Jack replied in his defence. "And I was *scared*."

"OK, it's OK. I'm just relieved that Lily and Greg found you." I looked up and gave them a grateful smile. Everyone was back now, apart from Jean Paul. And Vicky. Where were they? I put Jack down. "Come on, let's go and see if Dad's arrived."

Suddenly Jack started leaping up and down excitedly. "Look, Amy! Look at the top of the wheel. It's Jean Paul. Is he still looking for me?"

Jack began to wave his free arm and shout, "I'm here, I'm here!"

But I could see quite clearly that Jean Paul was not looking for Jack any more. Instead, he had his arms around someone in a tight embrace. And that someone was Vicky.

17

I walked back with Dad and Jack. I had to tell Dad about Jack getting lost. He was too young to keep secrets and it wouldn't have been fair to ask him to. To my surprise, Dad was concerned, but not angry. In fact he said I shouldn't be too hard on myself and that I'd been a great sister to Jack this holiday.

When we got to the tent, Mum was already asleep and Jack, exhausted by the drama of his evening, had crashed out in Dad's arms before we even got half-way home. Dad shook Jack's

flip-flops off his feet and laid him down to sleep in his shorts and T-shirt. I told Dad I was going to read my book, but as soon as he had gone I curled up on my camp bed. My head was spinning. I never would have believed that Jean Paul would do anything to hurt me. But he had. He knew I was frantic about Jack at the fairground, but when I looked up at that Ferris wheel, it seemed I was the last thing on his mind. I felt hot tears begin to well up and I buried my head in my pillow.

A short while later, I heard a familiar French voice softly calling my name outside the tent. I pulled my sleeping bag over my head.

After a few minutes, Dad appeared. "Erm … Amy, there appears to be a young gentleman outside who wishes to speak with you."

"Tell him to go away," I ordered from inside my sleeping bag.

"Are you sure? He seems rather *desperate* to see you."

"Well, I'm not desperate to see *him*."

There was a pause. "Right." Another pause. "OK, I'll tell him this isn't a good time, then."

I flung the sleeping bag off my head. "No, *don't* tell him it's not a good time, tell him it will *never* be a good time; tell him to go away and never come back."

Another pause. "Right," Dad said again and disappeared outside. I heard a murmured conversation, then silence.

Dad reappeared. "Well, he's gone."

"Good," I blurted out, trying not to cry.

Dad came and stood by my camp bed. "Are you all right, Amy? I don't know what's been going on, but he seemed like a really nice boy. And very keen to see you."

"I thought he was nice, too. But he's *not* a nice boy, Dad." Tears started to fall down my cheeks.

"Do you want to tell me about it?"

I shook my head. For Dad to really understand how I felt I'd have to tell him about the riding and how I told Jean Paul about Mitzi dying, and it would be too painful to go over it all again. I didn't want to admit that I'd trusted someone … someone I believed cared about me … someone I thought was special. Only to have it all thrown back in my face.

"No thanks, Dad, I'll be fine."

Perhaps I'd been a fool and Sasha was right. I am too much of a romantic dreamer. Maybe there isn't such a thing as THE ONE. Maybe you might as well go for someone you don't feel that much for. That way you don't get hurt. I needed to keep my distance from Jean Paul; it wouldn't be difficult as long as I avoided the pool and the stables. It would be Vicky's triumphant face that would be harder to avoid.

In the morning, Lily came round to pick me up as usual, but I got Mum to tell her that I wasn't feeling well. Mum and Dad tried to persuade me to come out with them, but I said I'd be fine. I just wanted a quiet day by myself. So they left with Jack. I tried to read my book, sunbathe, do a puzzle in the paper, but I couldn't concentrate on anything. The hours seemed to drag on for ever, and it was so hot that eventually I went and lay on my sleeping bag. If I went to sleep, perhaps I'd stop thinking about what had happened.

"Amy?"

"Lily?"

The flap of my sleeping compartment opened, and an orange head appeared around it.

"Why are you in here in the middle of the afternoon? It's boiling. I know you're not ill. You've missed the whole day at Teen Camp."

"You know why."

The rest of Lily came in and sat on Jack's camp bed.

"Was she absolutely full of it today?" I asked bitterly.

"Well, no. Not really. To be honest, Amy, she didn't say anything about it at all."

"She doesn't have to, does she? She must be *so* pleased with herself. Charlie was right."

"Charlie!"

"Yes, he asked me if I was worried about Vicky and Jean Paul spending all that time together, you know, all the private riding lesson stuff."

"You might've got it wrong…"

"How?! You saw them; *everybody* at the funfair saw them. What part of having his arms around her

could I have got wrong? If he'd been holding her any closer he'd have crushed her to death."

Lily sighed. "I suppose you're right. Look, Amy, I know how hurt you must be feeling. I really do understand. But you can't stay in here for the rest of the holiday. We can still have some fun."

"I'm not going anywhere where I might see her," I said, fighting back the tears.

"Well, I know she's not at the pool now. Why don't we go? It'll get you out of this place and we can talk some more. Please?"

"You're sure she won't be there?"

"No, she said she was going to the…" Lily went red and stopped.

"The stables. Well, of course, why wouldn't she? Let them get on with it; they deserve each other." But inside I felt the pain, sharp and fresh.

"Come on then, get your things. Time is running out on my swimming lessons and frankly you suck at teaching me…"

"I suck! You're the worst swimmer *ever*…"

"I feel today might be the day I get it…"

When we got there, Greg was lying on the grass

next to the big pool. I looked at Lily and said we'd have our lesson later and we strolled over. Greg immediately jumped up and offered to go and get us all drinks, which we gratefully accepted. Lily and I spread out our towels and lay on our stomachs in the sunshine, cradling our heads in our arms. I turned my face towards her.

"Have you snogged him yet?"

"Amy! Shut up!"

"Have you?"

"No, I did have hopes for last night at the fair, but…"

"You spent most of it looking for Jack, I know. I expect that spoiled the mood somewhat. Though obviously not for *everyone*."

"Don't think about that, Amy. As for me and Greg, it's the disco at the end of the week and I think we have what you might call … 'an unspoken agreement'." She smiled. Then she winced, "Sorry."

"It's OK, Lily, you can talk about the disco – just don't try and talk me into going. My social life is over for the rest of the holiday."

"Hey! What about *me*?"

"You've got Diane and Greg and Tom and Jed. And, er … Charlie and Finn."

"Not the same thing at all! Please, I'm begging you… After everything I've done for you, you can't disappear on me now. Teen Club's nothing like as much fun without you. I've got no one to laugh at!"

"Hi, Lily. Hi, Amy."

We looked up.

Vicky and Selina were standing over us. I turned my head away.

"Vicky!" Lily gasped. "I thought you were—"

"Change of plan," Vicky interrupted. "Coming for a swim, Lily? Seems we never see you in the water, do we? Well, except the paddling pool of course. Come on, come in. I'll race you."

Greg had reappeared, with Tom, Jed and Charlie.

I could see their feet. But I didn't move. I lay perfectly still. I was not going to speak to Vicky.

"No thanks," Lily trilled. "I'm not really in the mood."

"Oh come on, Lily, it's about time you joined in. I'll race you a couple of lengths. What do you say?"

NO. You say "no", I thought to myself. *You couldn't stay afloat for two seconds out of your depth.*

"I'm OK, thanks," Lily replied. "Maybe later."

"Chicken."

"What?"

"Chicken. You know I'll beat you."

"No, honestly, I just don't feel like it…"

Charlie grinned. "What's your problem, Lily? Scared?"

"No."

"I think you are…"

"I'LL DO IT!" I yelled, sitting up suddenly.

Everyone stared at me in astonishment. Vicky or no Vicky, I wasn't going to have Lily humiliated in front of everyone.

Lily reached out her hand and touched my shoulder. "No, Amy, it's all right. I'll do it."

I mouthed a flabbergasted "What?" at her. She ignored me, instead shouting up, "OK then, Vicky, let's go."

As she got up, I grabbed her arm and hissed, "What are you *doing*?"

She leaned down and whispered, "Don't worry, I think I've made a massive improvement. Really and truly. I think I can do it."

"Swim two lengths? Are you kidding? You can't swim two metres, let alone two lengths. You'll drown!"

"Amy, I really think I can do this. Honestly, just wait and see." And she patted my arm and wandered off to the side of the pool where Vicky was now standing.

"Do you want to start with a racing dive or in the pool?" Charlie asked.

"Erm ... in the pool, I think," Lily replied.

I sat up. I needed to be on hand to jump in and rescue Lily the moment she let go of the side. They were starting at the deep end. She was slowly lowering herself in. I got up and walked to the edge. As I did so I saw a figure standing watching on the other side of the pool. It was Jean Paul. My heart stopped and so did the rest of me, until a wild splashing sound brought me back to my senses.

"Lily!" I called down warningly, but I was drowned out by Tom shouting, "Ready! Steady! Go!"

I jumped straight in.

When I surfaced, the space where she had been clinging on to the side of the pool was empty. I took a deep breath and dived, opening my eyes under water and scanning the bottom. I couldn't see her. I surfaced again and took a huge breath.

"What are you doing?!" Jed cried.

"Looking for Lily! I can't find her!"

Jed, Tom and Greg all pointed in the same direction.

I turned to follow where they were indicating. Half-way down the pool I could see a figure swimming strongly towards the other end. I recognized Vicky.

"No, *Lily!* Can you see Lily!" I screamed.

"Here she comes," Greg grinned, shading his eyes with his hand.

I looked again. And there, speeding towards me, slicing through the water in clean, efficient strokes, was Lily. My jaw dropped.

"Wow. She really can swim," Tom gasped in an awed tone.

"Seriously, like she's in the Olympics or something," Jed added.

"Help me out," I said, holding up a hand. Charlie immediately reached out to grab me. When I stood up he put his arm around me and pulled me close.

"Are you OK?"

I flicked my eyes over to where Jean Paul was standing. I didn't move away. "Yes, thanks, I'm fine." When I looked again, Jean Paul had gone.

Lily slid effortlessly towards the side with a long, outstretched arm and touched the end of the pool. In the distance, Vicky had turned and had just begun the return lap.

I extracted myself from Charlie, stared down and fixed Lily with a level gaze.

She looked up at me with a sheepish grin. "Seems like you were a better teacher than you thought, Amy."

"Get out, please," I ordered firmly. "I'd like a word with you, if you don't mind."

Charlie whined, "Hey, don't go." I pretended I hadn't heard and dragged Lily into the ladies' changing rooms.

"What the hell was all that about?"

She raised her hands in the air. "What? So you taught me to swim."

"Lily, there is no way that I taught you to swim like that. It was obvious just watching you that you have been swimming for years and years. I don't get what's going on."

She was laughing to herself. "You should have seen Vicky's face when I shot past her."

"Lily!"

"Oh yeah, OK. Well it's quite simple really. I wanted to be your friend. After that first day you had one hundred per cent decided you weren't coming back to Teen Club. Which, to be honest, is turning into a bit of a feature of this holiday. So I knew if I wanted to hang out with you I had to get you back there. I felt bad about not being more supportive in the stables that first morning. When you asked me why I wasn't with the others that day, the swimming thing just popped into my head. The truth was I wanted to find out how you were after your fright with that horse. Then you said you'd teach me to swim and I said I'd only let you

if you came back to the club. And you agreed and that was that. And I loved our sessions with Jack. I was going to get good really quickly, but we had such a good time I decided against it. You are seriously the most patient person that I have ever met. I'd have drowned me ages ago."

"You're mad!"

"I know. Phew! Kind of a relief to have that out in the open. And thanks for saying you'd race Vicky for me. Especially when I know that you would rather die than be in the same pool as her. That took a lot. I appreciate it."

I shrugged my shoulders. "Took a lot to pretend you couldn't swim all this time, just to make me come back to the club. But I'm glad you did."

"You need to come back to the club again, Amy. You can't hide away from everything that goes wrong. You have to face stuff."

"Not this time. This is different. Everyone knows. It just hurts too much."

"Everyone knows what? Vicky's not talking about it. You don't have to be her best friend, you know. I'll be there, and the others. Come on, I've

swallowed more water than I care to think about in the cause of our friendship. We're going to the lake again tomorrow and this time I'd actually like to swim. Diane's leaving today; Greg's off with his parents sightseeing tomorrow. Please don't make me go alone with the smug friends."

"What's the point? Nothing good has happened to me since I got to this campsite."

Lily's face clouded. "Really, is that what you think? Seriously. Nothing good at all?"

I didn't say anything.

"Thanks a lot, Amy. In that case, stay in your tent, don't come to Teen Club with me tomorrow and enjoy the rest of your holiday all on your own. You won't get over what happened with Jean Paul by hiding from people. I'd like to have helped you feel better. I thought we were friends. Obviously I was wrong."

And she turned and stomped out of the changing rooms, slamming the door with a shuddering crash behind her.

18

"Isn't Lily coming today?"

Jack stared in the direction from which she usually arrived, whilst the jam he was ladling on to his croissant dripped on to the table.

"Not today." I was about to take a bite out of mine, but changed my mind; I didn't have much of an appetite this morning.

"Are we going swimming with Lily later?"

"Nope."

"*Awwww!* Why not? I love swimming with Lily – she's funny."

"Lily doesn't need any more lessons, Jack. She can swim all by herself now. *I'll* take you. I can take you this afternoon after your club. I'm not doing anything else."

I saw Mum and Dad exchange glances.

"But it's *better* when Lily comes. She gets it wrong all the time, and she needs me to show her how to do it properly."

I managed a smile.

He dragged his finger through the jam on the table and licked it. "Are you going to hide in our tent again today?"

"I was not hiding!"

"You didn't go to your club yesterday. Are you going to hide again today? Why are you going to hide again today?"

"I'm not hiding! I just don't … feel like going anywhere, that's all."

"Why not?"

Dad and Mum went extra still.

"Because I just don't. I just don't want to, er … see someone in my club. You wouldn't understand, Jack."

"Were they mean to you?"

I thought about Vicky and Jean Paul on the Ferris wheel.

"Mmmm."

"Is it a bully boy? I didn't want to go to school when Gavin Blair bullied me, but if you speak to your teacher, Amy, they will take that person to the sandpit and talk to them quietly and they will come over afterwards with your teacher and say sorry and be your friend again."

"Yeah, well, I wish things were always that easy to sort out, Jack, but it's a bit more complicated than that."

He took a couple of contemplative chews on his croissant.

"So you're too scared…"

"No, I'm not *scared*…"

"So why don't you go, then? Lily is your friend; she'll play with you. Is Lily still your friend, Amy? I like her a million times better than your other friend, Sasha. She pretends I'm invisible, or slimy. You still like Lily, don't you? She hasn't been mean to you or anything?" he finished anxiously.

"No, Jack. No. She hasn't been mean to me." I sighed and put my croissant down on my plate. "In fact she's been the *opposite* of mean to me. The very opposite."

"So why don't you want to be her friend, then?" His eyes widened.

"I do want to be her friend, Jack, and will you *stop* with the police interrogation. I do want to be her friend. I *am* her friend."

Jack sniffed and averted his gaze towards the top of the pine tree in front of our tent.

I looked at him and an awful truth dawned. I wasn't acting like a friend to Lily. She had been kind and caring since the first day we met. I, on the other hand, had been too wrapped up in my problems to think about anyone except myself. Now I risked losing that friendship.

"Thanks, Jack," I said, leaning over to give him a quick hug.

"Where are you going?" he asked, as I scrambled up from my chair.

"To see Lily."

As I began to race down the road I heard a faint

cheer behind me. I looked at my watch. If I didn't run faster than I had ever done before, I was going to miss the minibus.

I had to chase it up the road as it pulled away from the clubhouse, shouting and waving, but I made it. I was hauled aboard to raucous cheers. I had no more breath in my body and suspected I was as red as a tomato, but I didn't mind. I crawled into the empty space next to Lily, who was steadfastly contemplating the passing French landscape.

"I'm sorry..." I wheezed, "...about yesterday. I should never have said that ... you know, about 'nothing good'. It's so completely untrue."

She turned her head slowly towards me and held my eyes with a cool stare.

"You've been an amazing friend this holiday, Lily. A truly good friend. And I'm really glad we met."

She nodded.

"And you *are* right." I glanced fleetingly towards the front of the bus at the back of Vicky's head. "It's ridiculous to hide away for the rest of the

holiday. It won't make me feel any better. And I won't see *you*."

She nodded again.

"Are you going to talk to me?"

She blew out as if she had been holding her breath. "Phew! I can't do it. I need to practise."

"Practise what?"

"Holding a grudge. I want to so badly, but I can't do it, and also if I don't forgive you, I'll have a much more boring day. And I think they might call that cutting off your nose to spite your face."

"I really am sorry, Lily. I feel so bad that I hurt your feelings. You've been the most brilliant friend to me ever since I first met you. I've been selfish and rubbish and totally wrapped up in my problems."

"Well, yes, that's true, but I know that your feelings are pretty hurt at the moment." She glared ahead to where Vicky was deep in conversation with Selina.

"So, are we friends again?" I asked.

"Yes." She sighed. "But as long as you understand it's purely because I'm totally desperate and there's no one else available, OK?"

"OK."

I caught her eye and we both burst out laughing.

Then Pit, who had been sitting next to our driver, chatting on her mobile, turned round to speak to us. "Change of plan, everyone. The adventure park has had a cancellation and they've just phoned to ask if we want the slot. What do you say?"

There was a loud cheer. It had been terrifying, but also brilliant fun. Everyone was keen to have another go. Everyone, it seemed, except Vicky, who hadn't been the first time.

"What?! You can't just change the plans like that," she shrieked. "That's not fair. We've not got the right clothes or anything."

"You're all wearing trainers and that's all you need," Pit soothed.

"But I want to go to the lake," Vicky said firmly.

"Well, I'm sorry but everyone else wants to go to the adventure park, Vicky. You didn't come before; I promise you, you'll have a great time." And she turned to face the front again.

Vicky crossed her arms and complained loudly the whole way there. When we arrived she held us

all up by taking for ever to get her harness and helmet on, and then she climbed in front of me up the rope ladder on the first tree with all the speed and agility of a sloth. I wasn't too happy being right behind her, but Pit had called out our names in the order she wanted us to climb and I hadn't wanted to argue. The only good news was that Vicky had stopped whining. But then she stopped everything else as well. Right in the middle of the rope bridge.

"Get a move on!" Charlie yelled from over my shoulder. Since we'd got out of the minibus, he'd stuck to me like glue. And after yesterday at the pool, when he had briefly put his arm around me, I was in turmoil about what to do. He *was* good looking; Sasha would think I was mad not to go for him. But every bit of me told me he wasn't what I was looking for; it didn't feel right. But maybe there was no right. I knew what I had felt for Jean Paul was totally different. But look where that had got me…

"What's with the rabbit-caught-in-headlights expression. Get moooo-ving!" he yelled at the still motionless Vicky.

Could I *really* make myself like this boy?

"Come on, Vicky," Pit urged from the other side of the bridge.

"I can't," she whispered.

"What?"

"I can't move."

"Yes you can, come on," Pit encouraged briskly. "Just slide your foot and hand along…"

"No! I can't. I can't move. I'll fall."

"You won't fall, you'll be OK, and if you did you've got your harness on, so you'll be fine."

This did not help.

"I'm feeling dizzy."

Pit stepped towards her. Vicky screamed. *"Stop! Stop!* You're rocking it! *Please* get back!"

Pit stepped back.

"Vicky, you are quite safe, now just—"

"NO I'M NOT!" she yelled. "Somebody do something! I'm going to fall."

And all of a sudden, watching her from *my* end of the rope bridge, I remembered how I'd felt that first day at the stables. I knew what it was like to feel terrified – so terrified that you couldn't move.

Shouting out instructions was never going to work.

"Hey, Vicky," I called softly. "Hey, it's OK, it's fine, honestly, it's nothing to worry about. It's just a stupid rope bridge, that's all."

I stepped gently out on to the rope. She looked up in panic.

"Shhh ... shhhh ... look, it's fine. Shhh ... steady, steady. You just stay there. I'm not going to make you do anything you don't want to." I edged my way towards her, talking quietly all the time. Eventually, I managed to get alongside her.

"I'm going to put my hand over yours." I could see her white knuckles clutching on to the rope. "And then, if you feel you can, you just move along with me, very slowly back to the tree."

She shook her head. "I can't. You don't know how terrified I am of heights."

"But I do know what it's like to be terrified, Vicky. Remember that first day at the stables?"

She nodded dumbly.

"OK, I'm going to put my hand over yours now. Ready?" She nodded again.

"Good, you're doing brilliantly. Now I'm just

going to slide our hands along, just a tiny bit at first, hardly at all, OK?"

And slowly, slowly, inch by inch we got back to the tree, where Vicky promptly burst into tears.

When the instructor had got Vicky safely down to earth, Pit took us to the café in the adventure park and bought us each a cold drink and a doughnut. After checking that Vicky was unhurt, she left to check on the others. She had insisted they carry on with the instructors, much to Lily's annoyance.

I stared pointedly up at the trees and Vicky drained the rest of her drink, then began to tap her fingers on the table. The atmosphere between us was strained and awkward. She coughed. I turned towards her.

"Thanks," she said.

"Forget it." I turned away again. She smiled weakly.

"No really, you were, er ... great. Thanks. I'd still be up there, if it wasn't for you."

"No worries."

"Sorry about how I was, you know ... not so

understanding about the horse thing that day at the stables."

I raised an eyebrow.

She gave me a guilty look. "Perhaps I should explain something."

"No need," I snapped. "I'd rather you didn't."

"No, listen. I know we haven't been exactly best friends, I know we both liked Jean Paul..."

I rose to get up. She grabbed my arm and pulled me down. "No, hear me out, please. It wasn't what you thought, you know ... that night at the fair. And I guess it's been wrong of me to let you go on thinking it."

"I absolutely do not want to talk about this, Vicky. I really don't."

"I did like him, you know I did. And I was determined to get him. And it's true at the fair I was following him because I wanted to get him alone. I'd tried before, but it was obvious he liked you. I saw him climb on to the Ferris wheel – he wanted to get the best view of the fairground to see if he could find Jack, and before I knew what I was doing, I caught him up and jumped into the

empty seat next to him. Pretty stupid, considering how petrified of heights I am. He was very surprised, I can tell you, but I thought it would be my last chance to try to get him away from you. As soon as I saw the expression on his face, I knew nothing was ever going to happen between us. And then I realized we were going up higher and higher on that wheel and I started to panic.

"It stopped with us at the very top and I just lost it, and the more I panicked the more the seat swung to and fro, and the more I could feel it swinging the more I was flailing about. I was even trying to lift up the safety bar to get out. Jean Paul had to put his arms around me to pin me down and stop the panic attack. By the time they got the wheel started again and we got down, you had gone."

I took a sip of my drink to steady myself. "Why didn't you tell me this before?"

She shrugged. "Jealous, I suppose."

"Of *me*?"

"Oh, come *on*! Everyone likes you, and Jean Paul adores you – what more do you want me to say?"

Nothing. I sang to myself. *Nothing at all.* We could see the others heading back towards us.

"That Charlie's cute, isn't he?" she observed.

"What? Oh yes, very."

"And *he's* available." She had whipped a mirror out of her backpack and was applying some mascara. She stopped to frown at her reflection. "He *is*, isn't he?"

"Completely," I said. "Absolutely, completely and totally available."

19

"Stop fluttering your eyelashes."

"I'm practising for tonight."

"Well don't practise while I'm trying to put mascara on them, Lily. Unless you want to look like a clown."

It was the night of the disco and we were getting ready in the unforgiving strip lighting of the washrooms. We'd decided if we could look good there, we could look good anywhere.

"You don't flutter anything else, do you?" Lily commented.

"What? Hold still, will you — I don't want to smudge."

"You never say 'she fluttered her lips', do you?"

"Shut up, because I'm going to do them now." I put down the mascara and twisted up Lily's lipstick. Luckily for her, her mother wasn't as strict on this as mine and she had quite a selection.

I held her chin and got ready to put it on. Lily suddenly blew hard through her lips in that wobbly-lipped way that horses do. I leaped back.

"What are you doing?"

"I'm fluttering my lips."

I screeched and drew the lipstick away from her face. "Well, stop it! I've got your spit on me now. Stop making me laugh, Lily, or else we'll never, ever be ready." I tried again, then stood back to view my handiwork. "There, you look lovely."

And she did. She was glowing and healthy looking. She was wearing a green silk, embroidered halter-neck top and a denim mini that showed off her endless legs. She peered at herself in the mirror. "I do look quite good, don't I?"

"Gorgeous," I replied. "Totally irresistible. Are

you feeling nervous?"

"Yes, but in a good way. Are you?"

"I don't know. I don't even know if Jean Paul's coming. He probably thinks I'm hanging out with Charlie now."

"So you don't think he'll be there?"

I shrugged my shoulders.

"Mmmm. OK. So three hours getting ready, blow-drying your hair, doing your make-up, trying on seven hundred outfits; you do that every time you go out, do you?"

I smiled. "How do I look?"

"Let me see. Hair impossibly TV-ad shiny; eyes as blue as blue, shown up by perfect sun-kissed skin; crisp, white little cotton dress too cute to exist... How about Devastatingly Gorgeous? He'll faint with bliss as soon as he sees you."

She looked at her watch. "Well, this is it." She took a deep breath. We both stood side by side looking at our reflections in the mirror.

"Ready to venture forth, Amy?"

"I think so."

"Right, let's go. Our destiny awaits."

When we arrived at the bar where the disco was being held, the DJ had already started. Fairy lights had been strung up on the trellis outside. The whole place was buzzing with excited people of every nationality. Even the cool French girls smiled and waved and said "bonsoir". Greg was already there with the German boys and the twins. He came up to say hello. He was looking positively rock star-ish. He put a tentative arm around Lily. She opened her eyes wide at me. Her evening had begun. They headed off to the dance floor.

And then I saw Jean Paul walk in, dressed in a faded blue shirt and black jeans. He pushed his hair back and gazed around the room. Until he saw me and our eyes locked.

"Amy!" Someone grabbed me around the waist and span me round. It was Charlie, and Finn and Selina were giggling behind him. "Come and have a dance."

"No! No, really, I, I don't feel like it yet. I'll wait."

"Wait? What for? You can't spend your whole life waiting." He pulled my arm.

"No, really, Charlie. I'm happy just watching."

"I'll dance." Vicky had arrived, looking stunning in a gold T-shirt and black satin shorts.

Charlie looked her up and down. "*OK*, lady! Let's go."

Finn led Selina on to the dance floor, and Tom and Jed went off to talk to the Dutch girls. I was left holding my lemonade. I went to sit at one of the tables outside.

"Hello, Amy."

I looked up, straight into Jean Paul's grey eyes.

"Hello."

He sat down next to me. His shoulder touching mine.

"You never let me explain."

"I'm sorry. I know what happened now. Vicky told me."

"But this is bad. Vicky should not have had to tell you. You should have trust in me. No?"

"I know, I know I should have. But…"

"Why didn't you speak with me about this thing?"

"It did look bad, you know."

"Yes, I know this. But it also looked bad when I saw you and Charlie at the pool, and just now, but I have to trust what I *feel*." He pushed his fist on his chest.

"We shared something, that day together, something special, no? That cannot go away in a day. Not possible." He looked at me with serious eyes. "You do know this, too? I hope."

I nodded. And then we talked for what seemed like for ever. Then the music slowed, and he reached out his hand and led me on to the dance floor.

He pulled me towards him and put his arms around me. I rested my head on his shoulder, then I drew back to look at him. "I'm sorry I didn't trust you, but you remember everything I told you that day at the stables? That means I trusted you very, very much. You do know that, don't you?"

He smiled. "You think that I could be interested in any other girl when I see you riding like a … a wild angel."

I smiled back. He was looking into my eyes. "And you are no longer afraid. You have a brave spirit."

He was very close to me now. I could feel my heart beating. "Now I have a big fear that I must tell you. A big fear I have felt every day since I saw you sitting in the car with your brother."

"And what is that?" I asked. My mouth was almost touching his.

"What you might do, if I do this…" And he leaned forward and kissed me.

"Is it not beyond the worst to be back at school? I mean worse than death, worse than anything you could possibly imagine in your wildest nightmares?"

"I'm just about surviving it. How about you, Lily?" I curled up on the chair in my room and tucked my mobile under my chin.

"It's OK, actually. Weirdly, with my new-found snogging confidence and my new, *professional* blonde highlights, I'm suddenly Miss Popular. I'm still pining for Greg, though. We did all have such a great time, didn't we? Those days after the disco?"

"We did." I smiled to myself.

"Even the smug friends thawed out a bit. So, did all your friends have such exciting holidays?"

"Well, Sasha had a good time in the Maldives. Kissed every boy in sight, *obviously*."

"Are you jealous?"

"No! How could I be?"

"*She* didn't find THE ONE, did she? Not like you did."

"No, but I think she found Two, Three, Four and Five."

"Disgraceful. But enough about her. Brace yourself, I've got some mega-exciting news."

"Tell me."

"Next summer my dad has asked me to go out to America and stay with him! He's going to try and get me some work as an extra on the film he'll be doing. For three whole weeks!"

My heart sank. I tried to sound happy for her.

"That's great, Lily. But I thought you were coming back to the campsite with us."

"I am, you twit! As if I'd miss that! I'm going to America when I get back."

I breathed again.

"That's fantastic. You'll be famous in a minute."

"I expect so, and if I'm not, it'll be brilliant anyway."

The doorbell rang downstairs.

"Lily, that's Polly at the door, we're off to the stables now."

"It's great that you're friends again. I can't wait to meet her when I come to stay with you at half term."

I grinned. "You'll really like her, and I know she'll like you. We see loads of each other now that I'm riding again."

"How does Sasha feel about that?"

"She did find it hard at first, but now she's realized I'm not going to abandon her, that I can be friends with her *and* my old friends – we all hang out together at school."

"How's the play coming along?"

"Great! Baz came up at rehearsals today and told me that he thought I was really good."

"Ooooh! Seems I'm not the only popular one around here."

"Stop it, Lily. You know I only have room in my heart for one person."

"I do. You'd better get going... Speak later."

I could hear Mum talking to Polly in the hall.

"Bye, Lily and thanks..."

"For what?"

"For everything."

"Be off with you. Go and gallop about on your pony or whatever you do."

I put the phone down on the dressing table next to a framed photo. It was of Lily, Greg, Jean Paul and me sitting in the shade of the square in front of the café. Jean Paul had his arm around me and we were all laughing. Pit had taken it for us.

My mind went over all the special times that happened in those long, sun-soaked final days of the holiday. The day when Dad just *happened* to bring Mum for a walk by the stables and Mum's face when she realized that the girl cantering across the dusty paddock towards her was me. The happy afternoons at the pool, laughing when Lily beat me in every race. And, of course, a boy called Jean Paul.

Amy

I picked up the photograph for the millionth time to look at his face. We must have emailed each other a hundred times since I came home and we'd swapped loads of photos we'd taken, but I liked this one best. A year seemed an agonizingly long time to wait till we saw each other again. But I knew we could do it.

On the last day at the stables, I had asked his mother what the name "Amy" meant in French. She had smiled and replied, "It means someone who is loved. Very much."

When I'd had to say the last goodbye, Jean Paul had held me very close and said, "You know what my mother said earlier? About your name?" I had nodded. "It is true." And he'd looked into my eyes and kissed me and I never wanted it to end…

"Amy, what are you daydreaming about? Polly's waiting!" Mum called up the stairs.

I kissed the photo and put it back down on the table. I smiled. It's true I've always been a dreamer, but this summer had been better than even my most wild imaginings. I felt like the luckiest girl in the world. I had my good friends here, and I had

also made a brilliant new one. I'd met the boy I'd been waiting for for so long, THE ONE, and I'd never believed it would ever happen. And the best thing about *that* was that he'd been waiting for me, too.

"Amy!" Mum shouted.

Jean Paul and Lily. Those two had given me the confidence to ride again, and I was loving it. I caught my reflection in the mirror as I picked up my riding hat, and watched my face break into a broad smile. Life was brilliant.

I headed for the door. "Coming!" I yelled.